Also by Jay Thomas Willis

Nonfiction

A Penny for Your Thoughts: Insights, Perceptions, and Reflections on the
    African American Condition
Implications for Effective Psychotherapy with African Americans
Freeing the African-American's Mind
God or Barbarian: The Myth of a Messiah Who Will Return to Liberate Us
Finding Your Own African-Centered Rhythm
When the Village Idiot Get Started
Nowhere to Run or Hide
Why Blacks Behave as They Do: The Conditioning Process from Generation
    to Generation
God, or Balance in the Universe
Over the Celestial Wireless
Paranoid but not Stupid
Nothing but a Man
Born to be Destroyed: How My Upbringing Almost Destroyed Me
Things I Never Said
Word to the Wise
Got My Own Song to Sing: Post-Traumatic Slave Syndrome in My Family
A Word to My Son
Off-the-Top Treasures
You Can't Get There from Here

Fiction

Where the Pig Trail Meets the Dirt Road
The Devil in Angelica
As Soon as the Weather Breaks
Hard Luck
Educated Misunderstanding
The Cotton is High

Poetry

Reflections on My Life: You're Gonna Carry That Weight a Long Time
It's a Good Day to Die

Longing *for* Home *and* Other Short Stories

JAY THOMAS WILLIS

LONGING FOR HOME AND OTHER SHORT STORIES

iUniverse books may be ordered through booksellers or by contacting:

iUniverse
1663 Liberty Drive
Bloomington, IN 47403
www.iuniverse.com
844-349-9409

ISBN: 978-1-6632-0331-1 (sc)
ISBN: 978-1-6632-0330-4 (e)

Library of Congress Control Number: 2020913464

Print information available on the last page.

iUniverse rev. date: 07/24/2020

DEDICATION

To Rhonda who could have been my lady had I been secure enough in myself.

The natural inclinations of the universe will force you to confront your most horrendous fears....

CONTENTS

ACKNOWLEDGMENTS

I acknowledge thanks to all my teachers at the old Galilee elementary, junior high, and high school.

Thanks also to my professors at Stephen F. Austin State University; Texas Southern University; the University of Houston; the University of Illinois—Circle Campus; and Loyola University of Chicago.

They all provided me with the best education they could.

Thanks to my wife, Frances, for helping me with an occasional point of spelling and grammar.

ONE

Longing for Home

I retired several years ago and owned a modest two-story, five-bedroom, brick home, in a South Suburb of Chicago. On this night, I was lying there in my comfortable, king-size bed with a warm comforter. It was in December, almost Christmas. There were four inches of snow covering the ground, and it was about 20 degrees below. My 60" Samsung Smart TV was blaring something from a rerun of George Blumer on the Word Network. That's the way I chose to allow myself to drift off to sleep. I had a light insomnia problem. Most of my insomnia came from the fact that I napped during the day, and found it more difficult to get to sleep at night. It is said that one shouldn't go to sleep with the TV blasting, but that's the way I chose to do it. Not going to sleep listening to TV might be healthy for different people under different conditions. They say it is OK to go to sleep listening to music, as long as it's not too loud, but not regular TV programming.

Finally, I drifted off to sleep. I found myself on my way back to East Texas; a mostly rural area about 125 miles southeast of Dallas, Texas. My parents finally got running water and telephone lines many years after I had long since left the area. The roads were not kept up or regularly paved.

We didn't get a graded-dirt road until I was six years of age. Before that we had no electricity. Prior to that all we had was a three-mile trail.

After my mother and father were married, they spent time in a number of sharecropping situations in and around Hallsville, Texas, living in shacks on plantations. It was the best they could do. Some of their sharecropping situations were for Black landowners. Finally, in 1929 with a baby coming, my mother wanted to settle on a piece of family land and build a home. My father consented, so they built a tin-roof shack made of recycled lumber on a fifty-acre parcel of land that was handed down through her mother's side of the family. My mother and father couldn't afford new lumber, so they tore down an old house a few miles away, hauled the lumber by wagon, and built the house. New lumber in those days was a rare commodity. They didn't really have the money for new lumber. This was common in those days. They used what they had. Most people in the area existed under similar conditions. Since it was during the Depression, building materials were even harder to come by.

They built the house in the small-rural community of Hallsville where their land was located. The land was approximately three miles off the main highway. The land is west of this winding, two-lane, blacktop, curvaceous, hill-ridden road; about twenty miles south of Hallsville, and twenty miles north of Marshall. When my parents first got married there was only a three-mile trail leading off this two-lane, curved, crooked, hill-ridden stretch of main highway in 1929. There were tree limbs, creeks, and deep ditches along this trail. But they managed to transport the materials on a wagon and built the house. It is hard to imagine how they did this by wagon. When my older sisters and brothers were children, they walked to the bus stop at the end of this three-mile-pig trail. They walked through the mud, the dew, the streams, the grass, the ditches, and the overhanging tree limbs. I'm sure that not having a decent road contributed to some of them dropping out of high school and leaving home prematurely.

Each family did their part to help cut the weeds, remove the fallen-tree limbs, and whatever else needed to be done. In the early part of my childhood I remember helping to cut weeds from and to patch up the trail. In some places, ditches were as deep as a house; and you could only maneuver the trail with a wagon, a horse, or on foot. In some places even this was difficult. Before the graded road was constructed my relatives confined their travel to daytime, and even daytime travel was rare. There were always stories about wild men, wild animals, ghosts, and goblins along the trail. Along with these things simply navigating the trail could be physically dangerous. My dad once got drunk and fell in one of the ditches on a moonless night. He dislocated his shoulder, and had to wait until the next morning to get help. Some of the community people came to assist in getting him out of the ditch. It's amazing some wild animals didn't attack him.

At one time, say prior to 1955, the whole community in those days was connected by a series of trails. Though, the automobile by this time had been invented many years ago, but most folks still traveled by wagon or horseback. Diffusion and invention took place very slowly. This was a backward community. Everything was within walking distance. They had a general store and their own school. They bartered with each other for commodities. There were people in the community with at least some rudimentary skills. They didn't have to go outside the community to get things done. There were carpenters, blacksmiths, and bricklayers; though, most of the houses were constructed of wood. Most of the houses had chimneys or fireplaces. They built their own houses, butchered their own animals, grew their own food, repaired their own tools, built their own fences, and served as midwives for their own children. They also took care of their own animals. It was a self-contained, independent, and self-sufficient community. They lived a simple lifestyle. Medical needs were cared for by a series of home remedies. There were those who specialized in these home remedies. Though, the automobile had been invented for many years, there were few automobiles before they began to build roads. I have no idea why the county didn't begin to build roads earlier—possibly because of discrimination. It's the only explanation I can think of. It could be more complicated than that. Town was at least twenty miles away, and the only way to get there was on horseback, wagon, or hitch a ride with someone who had a car. We lived isolated lives as if we were eighteen-century prairie farmers.

At one time my folks didn't even buy groceries from the store like they later did. All they bought from a store at this time were things they didn't produce: things life salt, flower, cornmeal, sugar, other spices, and household furnishings. Everything else was purchased, grown, or bartered for in the community.

I found myself on my way back to East Texas for a visit. I heard things had changed, and I wanted to see the nature and extent of these changes. My undergrad degree was in sociology, so I maintained a natural curiosity about the way people and societies function. The trip was uneventful. I found that the roads were well paved, once I got to my old homestead. They had city water, natural gas, better telephone services, access to the Internet, and every convenience possible for a rural area.

Blacks had mostly left the area and moved to larger cities: some nearby and some faraway. Other groups had moved in and bought the property. No longer were the roads narrow and unpaved. People had moved in from other areas and taken control of the area. There were many beautiful brick homes standing where shacks once stood.

I visited one of my old friends who had moved to Chicago soon after graduating from high school. I never thought he would amount to anything. He stayed in Chicago several years; long enough to get a Bachelors' and a Masters' degree from the University of Illinois. He even worked a full-time job while getting his degrees.

He had come back to East Texas and built a big ranch: he had cows, horses, chickens, hogs, and other animals on his property. He even had a big fishing pond. He taught at one of the local high schools. He also had a spacious log cabin that had all the modern conveniences.

I pulled up to his door about 7:00 p.m. that evening. His wife answered the door. We all went to school together.

"How're you doing Craig?" she asked, "good to see you again."

"Find, Mary, how're you?" I replied.

"John is in the study. I'll get him for you. He's preparing a test for one of his classes," she said.

John came out from his study smoking a pipe, nothing like the John I had remembered, he had changed his style completely.

"How're you doing, my brother?" he gave me a big slap on the back.

"I don't have to ask how life is treating you. I can see it is treating you well."

"It's treating me OK. Glad to be out of Chicago. I couldn't have stood that much longer," John said.

"What do you do for excitement in these parts of the country?" I asked.

"I do a lot of hunting and fishing. Good clean fun. I'm going boar hunting tomorrow night. Wish I could take you with me. You'd like it; it's a lot of fun. We shoot them with a bow and arrow," John said.

"You had some children I recall. Where're your children?"

"My two sons live in southern California, and work for Microsoft. They love it out there, except for the fires, earthquakes, mud slides, drenching rains, and other natural disasters. What about your children?"

"I have one son. He teaches at Michigan State University. He always says he wants to get to where the climate is warmer, but he hasn't made a move yet."

"He'll get around to it sooner or later."

"How do you like it here? I asked.

"I love it. It's what I'm used to, and it absolutely agrees with me. I wouldn't live anywhere else," John said.

"Whatever happened to Carolyn?" I asked.

"That's was your old girlfriend? Last I heard she lived in Dallas, but I'm afraid I hadn't heard anything else."

"I certainly like your set up. It's just what I always wanted to build on my old homestead. Who takes care of the place while you teach every day?"

"I have a ranch hand who handles that for me. He lives on the premises and manages it on a round-the-clock basis."

"That's great."

"What keeps you from following through with your plans?"

"Nothing, really, It's about that time."

"Then I look forward to having you as a neighbor. Would you like something to eat?" he asked.

"No thanks. I'm in a hurry, but I appreciate the hospitality," for some reason I didn't want to put him out to that extent.

"Thanks for stopping by anyway."

"I must get back as soon as I can."

Somehow, I was envious of what John had built for himself, and felt like a failure in my own life.

"Good luck on your trip back. Good to see you again."

"Same here. See you when I get back this summer."

With that I headed for a local hotel. I could have stayed with John, but again, didn't want to impose on him. I stayed at the Holiday Inn in Marshall. I got up the next day and came back to see my cousin.

A cousin of mine, who used to be my running buddy, had purchased a parcel of seven acres. He had put a trailer on the land. A well-constructed paved road led up to his front door. I decided to stop by and see how he was doing. His car was parked out front, so I figured he was home. I knocked on the door, and he came to the door.

"Hey Bobby, how're you doing?" I asked.

"Things are going pretty good, I'm retired now, I worked for the Santa Fe railroad for twenty-five years," he said.

"Things have changed a lot since I was here last."

"Yeah, most of the old and the young have move on."

"How do you like it the way things are now." I asked.

"I think I like it better," he said.

He gave me a long list of people and where they had moved to. He also told me about all the people who had moved back to the area.

"That's good."

"Your sister Mary, who lives in Marshall, stops by when she visits the old homestead."

"Good, I'm going by to see them before I leave town."

They had built an interstate highway through the area with frequent exits. They had connected the road leading to our house with another road that was only a few miles beyond our house. Everyone wondered for a long time why these roads were not connected. This gave greater access to a small town not far away. People lived nearby, but no one lived at our old homestead, but a paved road led right to it.

I left my cousin's place and headed to Marshall where my sister lived. The new interstate highway was a much better travel experience than the old curvaceous, hill-ridden, and winding highway. I got off the interstate in Marshall and drove over a railroad track, then a hill, and finally to my sister's front door.

I knocked on the door and my sister answered. She seemed a little beaten by time and the elements.

"Hey boy, how're you doing, did you have a long trip?" she asked.

My sister always referred to me as boy.

"Yes, it was," I said.

"Would you like something to eat?" she was still following that old southern tradition of showing hospitality by offering a weary traveler something to eat.

"That would be good."

They had just barbequed the day before and had some ribs, hot dogs, hamburgers, and chicken; some fresh black-eye peas, potato salad, rolls, and some lemonade. I sat down and ate to my heart's content. Her husband was a retired mechanic and was off somewhere fixing someone's car.

"I guess you can see things have changed a lot around here. At the old homestead most of the Blacks have sold their land and move to the city, and other groups have moved in," my sister said.

"Yeah, I see it has changed a lot," I said.

"They have all the modern conveniences out there. We didn't have that when we were growing up. If it wasn't so far out, I would consider moving back out there and building a house. The only problem is having quick access to medical treatments. My husband and I frequently discuss the issue. There's plenty of good hunting and fishing out there: plenty of deer, and wild boar roam the countryside. Hallsville has the best school district in the country. Again, not like it used to be. Hallsville has even acquired a number of other stores and even has a grocery store."

We talked for several hours. I told her I had to be back in Chicago by late evening tomorrow for an important meeting, and I had to leave soon. She told me to come back prepared to stay a while when I had more time. I said I would and got on my way.

I had a pleasant drive going back to Chicago. It took me twenty hours of steady driving. I was a bit tired at the end of my trip.

I had a hard time waking up from my dream, but finally came back to reality. I woke up in my bed, realizing that I had been only dreaming. I actually hadn't visited the area since my mother passed away in 1989. I felt like it was necessary for me to visit the area if only for curiosity sake. One of my sisters had told me that other groups had moved in and built some beautiful homes in the area where my family and I once lived. I had always dreamed of making a full circle and moving back to the area one day. I entertained the idea of building a log cabin and enjoying my older years in a pristine and idyllic setting.

> *"We need someone to complete us
> rather than compete with us."*
>
> *"Without a loving, respectful, and supportive family,
> the individual will usually achieve very little."*

TWO

My Dear Carrie Ann

I had a dream one warm-rainy night in March. It was another dream about longing for the good old days. It was about a girl name Carrie Ann. Carrie Ann was one year ahead of me in school. I never paid any attention to Carrie Ann until I was a sophomore in high school. We went to a small-rural school, and everyone knew everyone else. We had the usual after-school activities. The activities were somewhat limited because of the size of the school. This dream came out of the blue, and I felt it was unusual for me to be dreaming about Carrie Ann. I hadn't seen her since her graduation from high school, but had often thought about her. She did read some of my books, and got in touch with me several years ago.

I had seen Carrie Ann around the school since first grade. One cool night in December we were at a basketball game. I saw her in her yellow slacks, white halter top, and with a white top that covered the halter. Her feet were perfectly pedicured, and every strand of her hair was in place. She had the perfect shape: 34-26-38. I didn't know if anyone was dating her, but she was sitting there with another girl. This girl was known to be her best friend. One never went anyplace without the other. I wasn't all that smooth but wanted to get to know her better. I didn't think I had much of a chance, because I was a year behind her in grade level, but decided to give it the old college-boy try. We had a general rule: to stay at or beneath your grade level when looking for a girlfriend. I also was not an athlete, was not in the band, or the chorus. These were the only extra curricula activities at the school. I did hold my own with respect to academics.

When I saw her that night something magic happened! It was like I was seeing her for the first time. She was five-feet-four, dark skinned, a pretty face, and about a C-cup. She was one of the most attractive girls at the school. I couldn't imagine why she wasn't attached to anyone. I decided to throw caution to the wind and approach her. I had no idea how she was going to react.

I knew she lived a few blocks from the school in a modest, wood-framed bungalow. Both of her brothers were good athletes: both were good at track and football. Her father worked at the aluminum factory in Longview, and her mother was a stay-at-home mom. There were also several other brothers and sisters. Her parents, to my knowledge, were upstanding members of the community. They always participated in community affairs and all the activities at the school.

My father was a janitor at the county courthouse, and my mother took on the duties of overseeing our small farm. Neither my mother nor father ever came to the school or participated in civic affairs. My parents never voted once in their entire lives. I rather doubt if we were counted on the census. We were invisible for all intent and purpose.

I had dated a much younger girl named Josie up to my sophomore year. I had to stop dating her because she didn't seem to be growing out of her immaturity. We had broken up for the last time when I began to notice Carrie Ann. Josie and I had been on and off since she was in sixth grade. We were more off than on. Finally, I couldn't take the situation anymore, even though I did like her a lot.

We lived twenty miles from the school, and it was difficult to get to and from the school for various activities, or to go other necessary places. Before my brother bought me the car, I was relatively isolated. My brother realized this fact and bought me a 1963 Chevrolet Impala for my sixteenth birthday: it was black with chrome rims, red and white interior—with bubble plastic covering the seats, dummy-tear-drop fog lights, and two pipes coming straight out the back. It also had a 348 engine that purred like a kitten and a five-speed on the floor. It was almost too much car for a sixteen-year old. Carrie Ann knew I had just gotten the transportation, and this made me more attractive to all the local girls. In our relative isolation it was a plus for any girl to have a boyfriend with a car. I was also rated fairly high on the school's honor roll. I also wasn't bad to look at and dressed in the latest fashions. I did have a slight stutter and was a little nervous. My friends gave me the nickname cool, because I tended to be nervous.

Carrie Ann was sitting across from me in the stands. I saw her and her friend and decided to move to where they were sitting. The basketball game was about over. I knew everyone called her Carrie Ann.

I was sitting with my cousin. We frequently came to games together and generally ran around together. He was a freshman. He refused to join us. He kept saying she was too rich for my blood. I joined Carrie Ann and her friend anyway, and left my cousin sitting where he was. I wasn't going to let anyone stop me from getting what I wanted.

"Hello Carrie Ann, may I joined you, and is it all right if I call you Carrie Ann?" I was aggressive for a young buck and nothing could deter me.

Even though I was somewhat nervous, and had a stutter, I was still aggressive with respect to young women.

"Sure, that's what everyone else calls me."

"Are you enjoying the game?"

"Yeah, were winning one for a change."

We were playing a lower division school and had them beat by twenty points. We usually weren't that good in our division with respect to basketball. The coach spent all his time and energy on football and baseball. Track and basketball were strictly extra curricula. We had one coach for football, basketball, track, and baseball. These were the only competitive sports at the school. We had approximately five-hundred students in the elementary, junior high, and high school. All three were in the same location.

I got right to the point, "Are you dating anyone, Carrie Ann?"

Her friend looked at me as if I was inappropriate, giving me a dirty look, and indicating that they should stick to the customary rules, that upperclassman should not fraternize with those below them.

"I'm not dating anyone at this school, but my boyfriend from Jefferson comes to visit me every Sunday."

"Good, I want to be your friend."

"OK," she acted surprised.

"How do you feel about me?"

"I never seriously thought about you, Luther."

I was delighted she knew my name. All the while her girlfriend maintained a frown on her face. Her girlfriend was light skinned with long-black-straight hair.

"I want you to give me some serious thought, because I like you a lot, and I'm in the market for a girlfriend."

It was awfully bold of me to be approaching her in the middle of the stands while people were watching the game, but I had no unordinary cares or concerns, and there was no shame in my game.

"OK, I will."

"First, I want to know if it matters that you're a junior and I'm a sophomore."

"Definitely not. My boyfriend dropped out as a freshman. That is not important to me."

"Can we go to the Cradle after the game?"

"Sure, we can do that."

I liked her already, because she had a pleasant personality, was amenable, and easy to talk to.

The Cradle was a local pub. I liked to dance and found out she did too. We went to the pub and danced until one o'clock. I then took her home. On the way home we struck up a conversation.

"I really like you, Carrie Ann."

"Luther, I'll be honest, I had never seriously thought about being your girlfriend, but I have liked you for a long time. I never thought you would approach me. Ever since you would go across the street for me at lunch time to bring me a sandwich, I began to like you."

There was a small store across from the school, and girls were not allowed to go across the street. I would sometimes bring Carrie Ann a sandwich.

"I want you to consider being my girl. As I said, I

like you a lot, and I believe we have enough going to get something started."

I could tell that Carrie Ann was much more mature than my previous girlfriend: Josie. The difference in their conversations were like night and day.

After I saw Carrie Ann that night, I decided I had to have her for my girl. Her boyfriend came to court her at her residence every Sunday evening. That's the way we courted in those days. I had to somehow get around that.

Carrie Ann and I started by seeing each other at school activities. Before long, I told her that I wanted to date her exclusively.

"I've been seeing my boyfriend since I was a freshman. It will be hard to let him go."

"I hope you can do so for my sake."

Carrie Ann thought about it for several months.

One day she told me, "I hope I'm not making a mistake, but I told my mom I was going to date you exclusively. She said it was the thing to do rather than string one of the boys along."

I was excited at the news, "You won't be sorry, baby."

"I hope not."

Carrie Ann was curious about my relationship with Josie but had never mentioned it before.

"You won't."

After school, one day I dropped her off at home, and she asked me, "What happened to you and Josie's relationship?"

"She was a bit too immature. I should have known someone in eighth grade would be immature. All I saw were those big hips and breast."

"Can you be a little more specific? I don't want to make the same mistakes."

"That's a matter of privacy. I have no right to reveal issues in our private relationship."

"If we broke up, would you say something negative about me to your next girl?"

"No way would I do that. That's why I won't say more than I have."

"Could it be that she wouldn't have sex with you? That's the rumor her brother passed around."

"It has little to do with sex. It was just a matter of her overall behavior and attitude."

By this time, it was near the end of my junior year and her senior year. One Sunday we had a serious conversation about our future. We had almost made it through two more years of high school.

"Just wanted to know," she said.

"What're you going to do with your life, any plans for college?"

"I'm lucky to get out of high school. I don't intend on going to college. I never figured college was my thing."

Carrie Ann was a brilliant girl but made it through high school with only a "C" average. I guess she really wasn't a serious student. Her parents gave her no motivation or expectation to attend college and let her know she was on her own after high school. Her only plans were to take what job she could find and get married.

"You graduate this year; can you wait for me?"

"I didn't know you were that serious about me, Luther," tears came to her eyes.

"Then I must have a serious problem communicating. I thought you knew I was very serious about you. What do you think the last two years have been about?"

"Don't be silly, I was being facetious, I just wanted to hear the words from the horses own mouth."

"If you want to hear the words from my mouth. I want to spend the rest of my life with you, baby."

"I feel the same way, Luther," again, tears came to her eyes."

"Wait for me until I graduate high school. We can then get married. I want to attend college. We can get an apartment near the college campus where I attend. I know it will be hard, but we can make it."

"That's fine with me. I can stay with my sister in Longview, get a job, and wait on you to graduate."

"When I graduate and go to college, you can get a job and help me until I graduate college."

I was there for her graduation from high school, and she was there for mine. I bought her a nice watch for her graduation, and she bought me an alligator brief case for mine. We supported one another. We saw each other when we could until I graduated high school. I visited her in Longview every Sunday while she worked until I graduated high school. She said she was saving money for my college, but I told her it wasn't completely necessary. The brother who gave me the car had vowed to support me in college, even if I had gotten married. He had always been my most staunch supporter. This brother came to my graduation and wanted to meet my future wife. My brother, myself, and Carrie Ann went to dinner at Johnny Casey's restaurant in Longview.

I made an average score on the ACT Test and had almost an "A" average in high school. I applied to a college not far away and was accepted. As soon as I graduated high school we got married and moved to Nacogdoches, Texas, the town where I was to attend college at Stephen F. Austin State College. I had already been accepted for the fall. She got a job as a secretary in the business department at the college, and I took a summer job at Kentucky Fried. My brother supported me through college as he had always supported me. My car was functional throughout my college career. When I needed a part for my car my brother would be sure to supply it. Carrie Ann also supported me until I graduated. We never had any major problems. I tried to get her to attend college, and I would support her for a while, but she wanted nothing to do with such a plan. All she wanted to do was to keep being a secretary.

When I graduated, we moved to Houston, and we both were able to get decent jobs: she got another secretarial job at Texaco, and I got a job with the Department of Human Services for the city of Houston.

Eventually, we bought a nice house, had three children, and lived out the rest of our lives in relative comfort in a small suburb of Houston. My brother was killed in a car accident, leaving a $200,000.00-dollar insurance policy, with Carrie Ann and I the beneficiary.

> *"The only good way to accomplish any task is to handle it one step at a time."*
>
> *"It's human nature for people to try and take advantage of you, but you must always check them."*

THREE

Pushed Beyond Limits

I had a dream several nights ago. I don't know what this dream was trying to tell me or what it was signifying. My understanding is that most dreams are not realistic, and are usually made up of fantasy—a wish fulfillment in our unconscious mind. So, this short story may not be all that realistic. I was lying on my couch, and suddenly I was in college at Wiley College in Marshall, Texas.

Before I moved to Memphis, Tennessee with my parents, after graduating high school, I lived in Hallsville, Texas with my grandparents, a town ten miles from Marshall, Texas. My grandparents were getting older and needed someone to help them out on the farm. As I got older, I was able to transport them where they wanted to go. I attended elementary, junior high, and high school in Hallsville, Texas. I was familiar with

Wiley College. I had hung out on the campus, and gone to athletic events on the campus. Many of the local people attended Wiley. Perhaps that's why the focus on Wiley. I was encouraged to attend Wiley.

I had a 2005 GT Mustang, and the year was 2008. An older brother had purchased the car for me when I graduated high school. I was now a junior in college. A guy who lived down the hall named Elliott was slightly jealous of me. He broke into my room and disabled my computer. Fortunately, I was able to fix the computer. After high school, I had a summers internship as a computer technician. I figured it was Elliott, because I saw him leaving my room one day. He was the only other person besides myself who had gained access to my room. I didn't have a roommate at the time.

I came into his room that afternoon after checking my computer. I figured he would try to damage my computer, because he didn't have one, and was jealous of me. I made enough money typing, copying, and sending Faxes, to put gas in my car and keep it running. I came into his room and challenged him. We were equal in physical attributes in most respects.

"What were you doing coming out of my room this morning?" I asked Elliott.

"I hadn't been in your room, chump," he said.

"You're lying, I saw you coming out of my room from the other end of the hall."

"You were hallucinating, my brother."

"I had to reload my computer, but you damaged it. If you come into my room again, I'm going to report you."

We were standing in his room. All of a sudden, I became angry, and didn't feel I could let him get away with such an infraction. What stunt would he pull the next time if I let him get away with this one? I snatched out my knife and cut him on the arm, before he realized I had a knife. I could have reported him, but thought I must handle this myself. In such a situation the law of the jungle sometimes operates. Black people learn to handle things themselves; since, it is sometimes hard to depend on the authorities.

He grabbed his arm, and yelled out, "You cut me Negro; what's your problem?"

"You know what my problem is. You had better stay out of my room or you'll get worst than that. And stay away from my car."

A week before, I caught him hanging around my car. He tried to hide, but I saw him anyway. It was a practically new car, and yet had some unaccounted for scratches on it that weren't there before. I left his room and went back to my room. I told him if he told about the cut on his arm, I would tell about his breaking into my room, damaging my computer, and putting scratches on my car. It came to mind that everyone who comes to school is not interested in getting an education. Some people only go to college because their parents want them to attend, and they have nothing better to do with their time. Sometimes they are angry because their parents sent them. Others figure to attend a few semesters to satisfy their parents and then drop out. I was a serious student, and in college strictly to get an education—like the average individual.

The next day, after Elliott put a bandage on his arm, he came into my room, pointed his finger in my face, telling me that I better not tell what he did. He had gone to the student health services and gotten a bandage put on his arm. It wasn't cut too deep, just a slash, but it did bleed more than usual. He told student health services that he accidentally cut himself with a sharp-pocket knife.

"If you tell on me you'll be sorry."

I wasn't worried about his threats: I was used to people making threats.

"Someone has to stop you; your jealousy has gotten out of control."

"I was only trying to get back at you for talking to my girl: Cherry."

"Cherry and I are only platonic friends."

"It seems more than that, the way you guys laugh and talk together. I've seen you with her on several different occasions."

"I don't care what it seems like. I told you what the situation is. Besides, you had no right to scratch my car, disabled my computer, and break in my room, because of my relationship with Cherry."

Elliott didn't believe a word I said. He was stubborn. School had driven him a little haywire. He was a sophomore. He saw he wasn't getting anywhere with me, and decided to send one of his boys around to see me. First, someone came into my room and completely destroyed my computer, about a week after the visit from Elliott. The computer could not be repaired. The door had a flimsy piece of glass right next to the handle. They simply broke the glass and opened the door.

Elliott had his friend come over to my room and talk to me. This friend had huge muscles bulging from his neck, legs, and arms. You could tell he was a weight lifter. He wanted his boy to take care of me. I'm not sure how far he was willing to go in taking care of me. I suppose he was trying to pull a gangbanger on me.

"Why did you cut Elliott," Marcus asked.

"Because he keeps fooling around with my things. This time he completely destroyed my computer."

"You had better be quiet about it, or I am going to mess you up, do you hear me?" Marcus looked straight in my eyes.

I was fed up with them thinking they could push me around. I was concerned about college but wasn't going to stand for this. My mother and father had great expectations for me, but I still wasn't going to accept this. This guy was six-two, 180 lbs., and strong as an ox—muscles everywhere. I was only five-eight, with a slender build, very little muscles.

Marcus made steps toward me, as if he was going to grab me. I knew I couldn't let him get his hands on me, or he could squeeze me to death. I had a sword that was a souvenir from the Civil War on the wall. It was handed down through my great-great-great-grandfather. It wasn't very sharp. I grabbed it from the wall and stuck him in the arm. The sword went all the way to the bone. I was trying to discourage him. He kept coming at me as if he wasn't fazed and was some kind of trained zombie. I then stuck it in his leg, going to the bone again. Again, he was barely phased, but I don't think he expected me to cut him with a sword. He acted like a man possessed.

My door was open. Another student saw what was going on. He ran and got the dorm-mother, and she came to my room. Marcus was standing there holding his arm, immobilized, and bleeding.

"What's going on here?" the dorm-mother asked.

She was careful to enter the room, and looked around in all directions.

"He cut me with a sword," Marcus was speaking as if he was in pain, that he was in the right, and that I had done something wrong to him.

I was still holding the sword in my hand, if there was any further encroachment on my space, I was going to do even more damage to him.

"What did you do to him for him to stab you? Wrap that arm and leg with a clean towel," Said the dorm-mother.

"Nothing, I was just talking with him," said Marcus.

"Put that sword down. That sword could be considered an illegal weapon," said the dorm-mother. "I don't believe you, Marcus. What's your story Charles?"

"It's a long story. Elliott has been harassing me: breaking up and disabling my computer, putting scratch marks on my car, and breaking into my room. He recently damaged my computer beyond repair. I have also been seeing a girl that Elliott likes. He was upset about that."

"Why didn't you tell someone? I'm calling Dean Smith. Both of you are out of control. You should meet Dean Smith in his office in a few minutes. I will tell him you are on the way. Can you make it to his office without security?"

"Yes, we can get there without security."

After calling Dean Smith, the dorm-mother said, "Dean Smith will meet you in five minutes."

"OK, Mrs. Johnson," we both said.

The dorm-mother looked again at Marcus, "Is that a serious cut? When you leave here, you had better go by student health services and get some medical attention. But this is even more serious; see the Dean first."

Even in his pain, Elliott was still making cracks, as we walked on the way he said, "I'm going to get you for what you did to me. You better stay away from the Student Center. If I see you there, I'm going to beat you down."

I didn't pay him any attention. I wasn't afraid of his threats. I knew we first had to get out of this situation.

We walked over to Dean Smith's office. The Dean was there and waiting. Marcus was still holding his arm, and on the way there he walked with a limp. You could tell he was in pain. He could have even been exaggerating somewhat.

Marcus and I both walked into Dean Smith's office.

"What's going on over in the dorm, Charles?" asked Dean Smith.

The school was small, and the Dean and the dorm-mother knew all the students by their first name.

"Elliott broke into my room and damaged my computer. He also put scratches on my car. I cut him on the arm, and he sent Marcus over to deal with me about it. I have also been seeing a girl that Elliott likes. When Marcus came over to my room and threatened me, I stabbed him.

"What's your side of it, Marcus?" Dean Smith asked.

"I just wanted to talk to him, and he stabbed me in the arm and thigh." Tears almost coming to the big-strong man's eyes; he wasn't so tough after all.

"Where's Elliot?"

Neither of us knew, and we didn't say anything.

Dean Smith said, "This kind of behavior is unacceptable for college students. Why didn't you guys come to see someone in authority?"

"I figured I could best handle it myself," I said.

"We were trying to handle it," said Marcus.

Dean Smith did some investigating. He talked with

Elliott: Elliott admitted that he was angry about me developing a relationship with his friend Cherry. He also admitted to damaging my computer, my car, and finally sending Marcus over to handle me. Dean Smith decided that Elliott, Marcus, and I should be expelled, he decided this was too serious of an infraction to continue or ignore. If he let it continue, someone was going to get killed. He said he hated to expel us, but he had no other choice. All three of us were permanently expelled.

We were all guilty of a serious offense. Elliott was guilty of destruction of private property; Marcus was guilty of felonious assault; and I was guilty of assault with a deadly weapon—if you wanted to push it.

"All three of you guys are expelled for the near future. Pack up your things and be out by the weekend. I will be sure you get any refunds coming to you."

I called my father and told him what happened. My father said I had no other alternative.

We packed up and were to be out by the weekend. I don't think it mattered to Elliott or Marcus, neither of them was serious as a student. It was hardest on me; I had a 3.0 GPA.

I saw Cherry, the girl that Elliott was upset about, the next day. The news had gotten around campus.

"I hear you got expelled," Cherry said.

"Yes, I did, along with Elliott and Marcus," I said.

"What happened?"

"Elliott was jealous of me and pushed me beyond my limits."

I didn't mention that part of his jealousy was over her. She probably had heard that through the grapevine.

"You should have reported him to the Dean," Cherry said.

"That was my mistake, but it's too late now. I got my refund and will have to vacate the campus by the weekend. My refund will be enough to get me to Memphis and beyond."

"That's too bad, I thought we were developing a good relationship. But I have to go, I have a ten o'clock class. Keep in touch," Cherry said.

I never saw Cherry again. I only saw her as a friend anyway. I also never saw Elliott or Marcus again.

I decided to apply to Howard University for the fall of the next year. I applied and was accepted. I obtained a job as a waiter in Memphis until the fall. I was able to obtain a Ph.D. in sociology in six more years. After I graduated Howard, I got a job as a social scientist with the State of Illinois in Chicago.

I woke up on the couch, wishing that I had attended Howard and attempted to get a Ph.D. in sociology, instead of trying one of the local colleges in Chicago. My wife said I must have been doing some serious dreaming. I got up, put on some clothes, and headed for my favorite activity: gambling at one of the local casinos. I was restless and needed something to do.

> **"Don't be afraid of change, for change
> is the only constant in our lives."**
>
> **"Either you're going to be in the forefront of
> change or be the victim of change."**

FOUR

Moving on

I graduated from the University of Houston in May
of 1974, with a Masters' degree in social work, and
emphasis on Clinical Social Work. At times it was a
struggle to get through the program, and I had used
every resource I had in order to complete the course of
study. I don't think my professors felt I had the potential
to be a Clinical Social worker. I had a slight speech
impediment, and thus a handicap to my profession.

Many of my relatives from East Texas had come for
the occasion. I got several gifts for my graduation. It felt
good on graduation day and was a promising day; it was
a bright, auspicious, and otherwise lovely day—as most
days are in Houston—about seventy-five degrees. Prior
to my attendance at the University of Houston, I had

picked up a Masters' degree in guidance and counselling at Texas Southern University.

When I graduated, I had no job offers at first, but soon received several offers: I received an offer from the Houston Independent school district, an offer from a family service organization in New Orleans, an offer from a mental health center in Oklahoma, an offer from a mental health center in Ohio, and one from a Chronic disease hospital in Chicago. For some reason, I was late sending out resumes, and late getting replies.

We lived in a one-bedroom apartment in the southeast part of Houston; a relatively new and modern apartment complex. The furniture was modern, and my wife kept the apartment neat and clean. We had two cars: a 1972 Plymouth Duster, and a 1973 Volkswagen Beetle. I always figured that upon graduation I would leave Houston if necessary.

My wife and I talked it over and decided we would reluctantly give Chicago a try. I had no close relatives or friends in the area and felt a change would do me some good. I had never been close to any of my relatives, and most of them were in the Dallas area. My wife didn't like the towns where the other jobs were located. We went for interviews in all of them. At first my wife really didn't want to move to Chicago either. She really wanted to stay close to relatives in Houston and the local area. I think her mother convinced her to give Chicago a try. To my wife, Chicago was the lesser of several evils. I'm not sure why I decided to give the chronic disease hospital in Chicago a try, rather than one of the mental health centers. After all, I had an emphasis in my curriculum on Clinical Social Work.

We took care of our business in Houston. There was not much to take care of and decided to make the trip to Chicago. We rented an eighteen-foot Ryder rental truck, and loaded our things on the truck. We even put our Volkswagen Beetle on the rental truck. We had a long drive to Chicago. My wife drove her 1972 Plymouth Duster, and I drove the stick-shift Ryder rental truck. I felt a call of the wild.

We left early on a bright, sunshiny Monday morning, about 9 o'clock in June. We said good-bye to friends and got on our way. After looking at a map of the United States, we had decided on the route. We would take Highway 59 out of Houston into Texarkana, Arkansas; then Interstate 30 into Little Rock, Arkansas; then take Interstate 40 into Memphis, Tennessee; and finally, Interstate 57 on into Chicago.

My wife wanted to stop on the way at a friend's apartment, near our old *alma mater* in Nacogdoches, Texas. I hadn't been on the campus since the night I graduated, but decided against physically visiting the campus itself. Her friend and her husband lived in a cozy little apartment in a cul-de-sac in the heart of Nacogdoches. We stopped, my wife had a bite to eat, and I had a drink. My wife's friend had married my old college roommate.

We had a conversation about old times.

"I thought I was doing it to death in college. How did you graduate ahead of me?" Louis asked.

Louis and I discontinued being roommates during my sophomore year, and I hadn't had any communications with him since then. Louis was promising, intelligent, motivated, with a good family background, good schools, and good teachers in his background. I came from uneducated parents, inadequate teachers, and an overall poor background. But I graduated in three years and a half with a "B" average. Everyone wondered how a student without promise was able to graduate before everyone else who had entered in the freshman class of 1966. It was now 1974.

"I put in some hard work during those three and a half years."

"Where're you moving to?" Louis asked.

"Chicago."

"A lot goes on in Chicago. It is one of the most violent cities in the United States."

"I won't be living exactly in the city. I'll be living in a South Suburb of Chicago."

"You had better watch yourself in Chicago."

I had heard all the negatives about Chicago from other friends, relatives, and associates that I had talked to prior to making the move.

I think he was trying to discourage me from moving. He knew his wife and my wife were close, and it would be devastating for them to be so many miles apart. They had actually been roommates for a while. My wife had a lot of reasons for staying in the area. We sat and talked for a while, and then we got back on the road. Nothing and no one were going to discourage me from my destiny.

The weather was good every mile of the trip. There was nothing but sunshine and blue skies. At first, I kept pulling over at the weigh stations to weigh the truck and its contents. I soon came to understand that it wasn't necessary for such a small truck. Finally, I got the idea. We pulled over to rest on several occasions. Mostly, the only thing we stopped for was rest and to get gas.

Things were going well until we made it to what I refer to as the Cairo Bridge in Cairo, Illinois. At the time it was a winding gyro. My wife took one look at it, refused to cross it, and suggested we find an alternate route. We tried an alternate route, and it took us out of our way. I became alarmed when we came to an overpass that would only allow a thirteen feet truck to pass, and our truck was fourteen feet high. But this road was the only way I could see that would take us where we wanted to go. We then had to take another route. But we did get back on track after a while. It seems that we were headed for Kentucky. We got nervous for a while. In Evansville, Indiana we realized we were off target, and took Highway 80 and got back on Interstate 57. In

Effingham we knew we were back on the right track, decided to get a room for the night, and get an early start the next day. I believe her reason for taking the alternate route was to try and get me to turn around and go back to Houston. She kept telling me God was trying to tell us something. I felt like telling her that she was the one responsible for us getting off track, but I didn't say anything.

That night my wife tried to get in a final blow against making the move. She was doing everything she could to keep from moving to Chicago.

"You know I've never been more than a few miles away from my relatives. It'll be hard for me living all the way in Chicago," my wife said.

"You'll get used to it. At some point a bird has to leave the nest," I said.

"What do you know about Chicago anyway?"

"Not a lot. It's like any other American town. I spent some time there when I was in the Navy,"

"What if something happens in my family? It'll be hard to get back and forth."

"Planes leave Chicago for Houston every day, on every hour, and vice versa."

"But that's a lot of hassle. I wanted to always be within driving distance of my parents."

"We'll see how things work out in Chicago. I make no promises, but we'll see."

My wife didn't seem to realize that we live in a highly

mobile society, and individuals can't always live near their parents. Jobs are often scattered across the country.

"If things don't work out will you promise to move back to Houston?"

"I'll certainly consider it."

"What if I can't find a job?"

"You won't have a problem finding a job in Chicago. Plenty of hospitals need someone with your skills."

"I hear they're very cliquish in Chicago, and that you almost have to know someone to get a decent job."

"It's not as bad as all that."

"But how do you know, you haven't lived there for any length of time."

I couldn't believe how my wife was trying to find every excuse she could for turning around at the last minute and heading back to Houston. I hadn't realized how attached she was to her family. I guess I didn't know her as well as I thought. But we had come too far to turn around at this point. I went to sleep and dreamed about my work situation.

It was my first day on the job, and some of my wife's hesitancy about Chicago was creeping into my own mind.

My employer said, "We made a mistake. I forgot to ask you who was your sponsor. This is a county facility, and everyone has to have a sponsor."

"What do you mean?"

"You must have a political sponsor: a Precinct

Captain, a Block Captain, a Ward Committeeman, a State Congressman, a U.S. Congressman; someone on that order."

"Nothing was mentioned about this when I interviewed."

"That's the way we do things in Chicago. I'm afraid before we hire you will need someone to sponsor you."

"But I just came from Texas and don't know anyone."

"Start with your Block Captain and see if you can get someone to sponsor you. It shouldn't be that much of a problem."

"You can't hire me until then?"

"That's right, and it shouldn't be that much of a problem to find a sponsor."

I looked around for weeks, and still couldn't find a sponsor.

My wife said to me, "I told you how things were in Chicago."

Potential employers told my wife the same thing, that she needed a sponsor. We looked for jobs for a month but still couldn't find a sponsor. I decided that things might be better in Texas and packed up and moved the next week. My wife was elated. At that time, I was almost out of funds.

The scene shifted, and I went right into another dream. My wife's sister was on her death bed, and she was dying of cancer. My wife got a call from her mother. This was soon after we got to Chicago.

"Sherrie is breathing her last breath. If you don't get here to see her you may never see her alive again."

"What's wrong with her?" my wife asked.

"The doctor said her cancer was in the last stage."

"But she was doing fine last month."

"Apparently, she had it but she had no idea she had it. It metastasized and got out of control all of a sudden, before she knew she had it."

Since she was so young, she never considered she would have cancer, and hadn't visited the doctor since her last checkup, one year ago.

"OK."

"Can you come and see her before she takes her last dying breaths?"

"I don't know. It'll be hard for me to make the trip right now. I'm afraid I'm out of funds and can't afford the trip. It took all of our funds getting settled in Chicago."

"Try to get here if you can."

"I'll also have difficulty getting off from my job. Employers don't take kindly to giving people time off, after only being employed a few weeks."

"If you can swing it, I'll send you a ticket in the mail."

"I'll see what I can do and let you know."

I can see why they were so close. My wife had always been able to depend on their support. She didn't want to leave the area, because it would threaten her support and security.

"Don't wait too long. Sherry doesn't have that much time to live."

"I'll do what I can."

My wife came to me crying, and I woke up from my dream. Again, glad it was only a dream. I woke up in a cold sweat, but glad that I was only dreaming. We got a good night's sleep and got back on the road the following morning about ten o'clock. Again, the weather was sunshiny with blue skies. The sun was so bright I knew I had to wear shades in my future. It was a gorgeous day, about seventy degrees. It was a straight shot into Chicago from here on out. We drove until that afternoon, and finally arrived at two o'clock. I drove until I saw a sign that said Sauk Trail. I knew I was there.

We had no problems and rolled into the south suburbs on a cool, sunny, bright Wednesday afternoon. We were ready to withstand the tide, for better or worse.

I had already reserved an apartment when I came for my job interview. I went by the apartment rental office, and they said they were a little behind, and the apartment hadn't been cleaned. I had only applied for the apartment the previous week. We had to wait until the apartment was cleaned. My wife kept saying the apartment not being cleaned was an omen, and that she told me we shouldn't have come. They did clean the apartment, and we moved in with no other problems. This was her last effort to get us to go back to Houston.

We unloaded and unpacked. My wife's cousin who

had lived in Chicago for a number of years came over with a friend to help us unload and unpack. I then took my rental truck around the corner so I could get my Volkswagen off the truck. It was easy to do. Ryder had a convenient loading ramp. My wife found a grocery store right around the corner also.

Two days later I went to work and was settled in for my stay in Chicago. Two weeks later my wife was able to secure a job. We would spend many years in the south suburbs. My only regrets being the snow and ice that comes each winter.

> *"To the universe we are all kings, queens, and noblemen."*
>
> *"It's not where you come from but where you are headed."*

FIVE

Blue Bloods

I first met Elsie in the hills and hollows; the wild and wooly country of East Texas. I don't remember exactly where I first met her, we lived in proximity, and there were many opportunities. Some Black students from the town she lived in were attending our school temporarily; until the local school decided to integrate. Our school was twenty miles away from her small-rural community. The Black school in her community only advanced as far as the tenth grade, and the students who had wanted to continue their education further had to go to another school twenty miles to the south. Some of the students would end their education with the tenth grade, others would travel the twenty miles to finish their education. It was the same system which educated my mother, but my mother only graduated the eighth grade, because back then the Black school only went to the eighth grade. The system was designed to further limit the education of Black students. It was another example of systematic discrimination against Blacks. But this year the students who had graduated tenth grade came to our school.

My brother had purchased me a 1962 Chevrolet Impala, black and sleek with chrome rims, black interior encased in bubble plastic, and two tail pipes coming straight out the back. It had a 348 engine that purred like a kitten and a five-speed on the floor. My brother was generous to me in that way. He also made sure that I kept cash in my pocket. I could go wherever I wanted. My parents placed no restrictions upon my itinerary. For some reason, I decided to go to a basketball game at the school in the local town where the new students at our school had transferred from, to see Elsie play basketball. Her cousin had told me she was on the team. I was interested in her.

When I saw Elsie play, I thought she played with such grace and style, that she captivated me. She put on a show all by herself. It was like she was the whole team. She didn't make many points but had a unique way of bringing the ball up the court. She had a strut like a gamecock and was as majestic as a lion in the jungle.

Her parents were well educated: her father was the principal of the local school, and her mother was a teacher at the school. They had a nice, modern, and comfortable bungalow in their community; the family was known for miles around, and well thought of. Elsie's parents were upstanding pillars of the community and had great influence in the community.

Elsie was a classy girl with a lot of charm, grace, and style. She wasn't all that beautiful, and her body wasn't all that perfect, but she dressed well. She also kept her coiffure neat and trimmed. About 28-22-30, stood five-feet-five, and weighed about 115 lbs. I liked something about her style and the way she carried herself. Even then I was attracted to someone who was ambitious. I was ambitious myself and wanted to always be headed in a positive direction. I also wanted to be associated with someone who dreamed big. This girl represented everything I wanted to be associated with. I wanted all this even though I came from nowhere and was a nobody. I'm not sure where I got my high-minded ideas from, but I had big ideas for sure.

Again, I'm not sure why I was ambitious. My parents lived in a shack at the end of a red-dirt road. I came from an uneducated family. We all lived in rural areas, far from a small town. My mother only graduated the eighth grade, and my father dropped out in the second grade to help on his family's farm. My parents were once sharecroppers on a Black man's place. Now they had their own small farm. I had four brothers and five sisters. Only four of my brothers and sisters graduated high school. Considering her background and mine, I don't know what made me think I could be close friends with Elsie, yet, there was always something in me that made me strive for things I perceived to be on a higher level. Looking back on it, I found myself outclassed, outmaneuvered, and outgunned in too many situations—especially with respect to girls—but that didn't stop me from trying. I liked them classy and well-bred.

I was ambitious partly because God had blessed me with being able to observe some ambitious people in my life. But I had also seen some derelicts in my time. I tended to identify with the upwardly mobile and well-to-do individuals that I had known in my life. One of my brothers also encouraged me to work at developing my potential in every way I could.

I never will forget, there was a young man who lived down the road from me, and Elsie had several older sisters. I would go places and see Elsie's sister and this young man together. They always seemed to be having such a good time. For some reason, I didn't see how he could have her for his own. I knew where he came from and knew something of her background. I wondered, how the hell did he have the gall to parade around with her on his arm. I mean, who did he think he was. I realized I was only jealous of him. I couldn't see why the older sister would even talk to this character, but the guy was no worse off than I was, and here I was trying to make time with the younger sister. An excellent example of the pot calling the kettle black. The sister was a cute girl about five-feet-three, and 120 lbs., always neat and well presented. Her coiffure was also always together. I used to wish I could have been this guy, and I wondered what special charms he possessed. He was just an average guy trying to make it in the world. I would watch them closely as they paraded around, whatever the venue. He was no better than me, I thought, except that he didn't stutter, and was not as nervous as I was. I did have a car and he didn't, so I called it about even. No one in the community was much better off than the other, except for the few teachers that lived there. My parents and his were about on an equal par.

I had seen Elsie in the city of Marshall, at funerals, and on a number of other occasions; but never stopped to chat with her or pay her any attention.

One night I went to a game at Elsie's school. Her cousin had encouraged me to go to the game. She was playing in the game. After the girls played their game, I walked around in the stands to where she was sitting. I approached her. I got stares from all the community people, as if I was doing something inappropriate. People looked at me as if to say, don't you know who her father is, he will kill you. But I was big, bold, bad, and bodacious. I was actually a little nervous, but I didn't make anyone aware of it. I could manage my impressions fairly well.

I approached her in the stands.

"Hello Elsie," I sat down beside her.

"Who're you and how do you know my name?"

"I'm Brent from Hallsville. I go to school with Craig and Debra."

Craig and Debra were her cousins who had transferred temporarily from the local school. Craig and Debra played basketball at our school. Craig was seven-feet tall and two-hundred-fifty lbs. He was an exceptional player.

"So, that's where the students went."

"Yeah, all the students are in my class."

"I might come there in two years if the school here doesn't integrate."

She had a positive attitude, was friendly, and amenable. Even though she tried to be friendly, she had a way of looking down at you from on high. I believe this was just a part of her aristocratic training. But I had grown to admire a girl with a little bit of sass and superiority. I figured we could work through all that. I was happy just to know her, even though I could feel her superiority dripping from her like ice cream from a cone on a hot summer day.

"Then I hope they don't integrate, and you come sooner rather than later. I would love to have you at our school."

I never stopped to consider that by the time she transferred I probably would have graduated. I figured her to be a freshman. The buzzer sounded and the game was over. The boys had won their game by ten points. The boys seem to also have a good basketball team.

"Walk me to my car," she said.

"Are you sure your father won't mind?"

I had heard some nasty things about her father with respect to his daughters. I was observing her while she was playing. My friend, a guy who I usually traveled with said, "Get that look out of your eye, her father doesn't play when it comes to his daughters."

"What do you mean?"

Knowing full well I knew what he meant.

"He doesn't like young men trying to fool with his daughters."

My friend had previously lived in the community, went to Elsie's school, but had moved to the community where I lived.

"I'm not worried about her father," I said.

I figured what could he do except tell me not to see his daughter.

"Those are famous last words," my friend said. "He has run any number of young men away from his house."

"But we're not at his house."

"Then, you have been cautioned, proceed at your own risk."

Elsie and I resumed our conversation.

"He won't mind," she said. "My father used to be protective but has changed over the years. He is not as hard on me as he was on the older girls."

We walked out of the gym and toward her car.

"What grade are you in this year?" I asked.

"I'm a freshman, what about you?"

"I'm a junior."

"Good, I like upperclassman."

"Do you have a boyfriend?"

"That's a new concept for me. Up to this point my father hasn't allowed it. But my mother and I had a good talk with him. I think he will change his mind about allowing me to date. It's hard to get old-fashioned ideas out of the heads of some adults."

"Tell me about it. My parents are exactly the same way."

Her father came up to the car, "How're you doing young man?"

"I'm fine, sir."

"That was a good game Elsie," her father said.

"Don't tell me that; I didn't hit very many points. I don't consider it a good game unless I make at least ten points."

"You still played a good game."

"Did you enjoy the games, young man?" her father asked me.

"Yes, I did, sir."

Elsie's father looked at her as if it was a signal that it was time to go.

"We have to go. I don't want to be guilty of holding him up. He will chastise me later if I do."

"OK, Elsie," I said.

"Do you know where I live? Come by to see me on Sunday, and test my father out concerning my freedom."

"By Elsie, see you on Sunday."

I didn't like the idea of being used as a guinea pig, but I wanted badly to see her, and to establish my right of visitation on a regular basis.

I never thought I had much of a chance with Elsie but decided to give it a good try. In my young days I saw no such thing as class. I didn't ever consider being outclassed. We were just two young people trying to find our way through the rage and the storm. I liked her style, and that was all that mattered to me.

I couldn't wait until the next Sunday. I washed and waxed my car, got a haircut, and bought some new cologne and deodorant.

I arrived about four o'clock on Sunday evening. I knocked on the door and her father answered.

"Yes, who do you want to see?"

He knew full well who I wanted to see.

"Elsie," I said.

"Elsie is not allowed to receive company at this point," he said.

"Sorry sir, I didn't know that."

"She should've told you. Talk to her when you see her, and she'll let you know when she can start receiving company. We talked about it, but I hadn't reached a definite decision."

I personally knew she was seeing her older sister's husband brother. I figured they were just friends and it wasn't that serious. Her sister's husband was the coach of another local high school basketball team. I didn't have much going for myself, either family wise or personal wise. With me, what you saw was what you got. Everyone around for miles knew my family well. I couldn't escape my family background.

Elsie didn't come out, and I never saw her again. I didn't at that point have a phone. It was difficult for me to call her. I soon went away to college and lost complete contact with her. Several years later, I heard she attended a local college and eventually got married and moved to Dallas. I hope she did well for herself. In the back of my mind, she was one of those who some people would say, was too rich for my blood anyway. My mother would sometimes tell me that I was always shooting for the stars and trying for the impossible. I suppose it's not a bad way to spend one's life, even though one might be in for a lot of disappointments.

The schools in that small town did integrate the next year and accepted all the students. We too often see discrimination as the cause of people's behavior, when sometimes there are other reasons. The next year Elsie played basketball for the town's team and was the star player. I heard about her through the grapevine.

I went to college with her cousin Craig. He played on the college basketball team. Craig and I ran in different circles, and I rarely saw him on the campus. I meant to ask him how Elsie was doing and what was happening with her, but I never got the chance. I graduated from college, moved to Chicago, and lost all contact with the people in East Texas. As they say, out of sight, out of mind. I wasn't trying to put the people in East Texas behind me, but simply felt that it was time to move on to greener pastures.

I often think about her, as I do about many of the girls in my past, but not in a serious way. I simply wonder what the situation could have been.

> *"Most people don't like or dislike you because of your race but because of your personality."*
>
> *"I can't hear what you say; because, your behavior is louder than your words."*

SIX

Cajun Queens

I was born in a small-rural town in East Texas called Hallsville. I spent the majority of my young years ploughing a mule on a dirt farm from sunup to sunset. Yet, I managed to graduate high school, went to college, then to the military.

I got out of the military in 1971, a few years before the Vietnam War ended, on a warm spring day in May. The war I believe ended in 1975. I came directly to my brother's apartment in Third Ward in Houston. Even after college and the military, I had no other place to go except back to my parent's farm, or to live with my brother Henry in Houston. I had four brothers and five sisters, but we were not a close family. I had seen a lot of discord between family members when one tried to live with the other, and I wanted no part of such disagreements. My parents had no telephone or indoor plumbing. I didn't feel I could get use to not being able to take a shower. They also lived twenty miles from a small town in either direction; I would have to walk a three-mile, red-dirt road to get to the main highway. In the country, I would have very little chance of obtaining a decent job. My parents and no one else could help me purchase a vehicle, or in any other way. In addition, I had gotten used to being in proximity to cities, and didn't think I could get use to rural living. I had no cash. I should have saved every paycheck while in the military, but I was living wild and fancy free, trying to enjoy myself, and didn't look after my money well. After being in college, I had denied myself for too long. I guess I will never learn. Going back to that farm was the last thing I wanted to do. If I had gone back to the farm, I would have been stuck in the middle of nowhere without transportation. I hadn't communicated with Henry in quite a few years, and we had long since gone our own separate ways. But I figured he could offer me a place to live until I could get on my feet—so to speak. Henry was known to have lived an unstable existence for the latter part of his life. But he was the only alternative I felt the least bit comfortable with at the time.

He lived in an apartment at 1519 Palm street; it was right off Almeda street, one of the main streets in the area. A quiet little neighborhood. It was a little house with an apartment over a garage, with a screened-in porch sitting to the side. It seemed that in its heyday the apartment was used as a servant's quarters, and the houses in the area were really once beautiful spectacles to behold. The apartment was a decent little apartment with pine wood paneling throughout. It could have been a better apartment with a little fixing and cleaning. Henry wasn't conscious enough to keep up the appearance of the apartment. He seemed to be able to appreciate deteriorated conditions. That's the way he seemed to have come to be conditioned over the years.

Henry was forty-years old and had lost some of his enthusiasm and zest for life at an early age. At one time he would have taken better care of his apartment and his life, but at this point he didn't seem to care. He rarely paid his rent on time, and the landlady had to chase him down to get her money. He would make a game of it. Henry was known for changing jobs, cities, and apartments quite frequently. He did this to escape the demons that were chasing him, and the spells and hexes people were trying to place on him.

He had a habit of associating with some of the most negative and notorious characters in the city. He seemed to feel comfortable around these people. One particular character believed in voodoo, spells, and magic. It is quite common for certain elements in the Black community to be superstitious and to believe in the supernatural. If you can't control the forces around you what else are you going to do. Festus would at times come to live with Henry when other of his friends got tired of his foolishness. He would sometimes walk around the apartment making incantations, burning candles, casting spells and talking to himself. Most of his teeth were missing, and his head was bald. He seldom took a bath. For some reason Festus and Henry were attracted to one another. I believe their similar views about voodoo drew them to one another. Henry would burn candles and visit the voodoo lady to remove any hexes or spells placed on him by negative people who didn't like him and were out to get him.

Henry didn't have a lot of friends, but I remember Carl, a friend who went in and out of jail. In the meantime, Carl was able to do construction work with Henry. That's how they got to be friends. I got to know Carl's sister-in-law, but the relationship didn't last long. I don't think I was what Beverly wanted, nor was she what I wanted. Because I was fresh out of college and the military, and somewhat deprived, sex was the only thing I was interested in at the time. We eventually quit seeing each other completely. Carl ended up writing a series of bad checks and went to prison.

Henry would, when I was much younger, support me in every way he could. He bought me a car and gave money when I needed it. He would even come by the farm to see me on an occasional visit. He even gave me emotional support. But at this point all that had changed; I guess because both of us had gotten older. I guess he considered that he had planted his seed, and his role had ended. Henry got off from work after getting paid, and claimed that someone hit him in the head, and took his money. He ended up in Ben Taub emergency room. I believe he staged all that, got someone to hit him, and faked that someone took his money, so he wouldn't feel any responsibility or guilt for not giving me any money. I didn't expect any money from him anyway. I believe his friends convinced him to pull off this little scheme.

I also believe he disconnected his phone so I wouldn't run up his telephone bill. There was a phone there, and there was a plug, but it wasn't plugged in. Later, I distinctly remember seeing Festus operating the phone. It was the only conclusion I could reach.

Once Henry had some meat patties for a dog in the refrigerator. But he didn't own a dog. I figured out early what Henry though of me, yet, it took me a while before I decided to make a move.

Henry had another friend who was a drug addict. Leonard also worked with Henry. Leonard would get paid and not show up at home for several days, while leaving his family to fend for themselves. They never could keep an apartment, because Leonard wouldn't pay the rent consistently. That's how I met Alicia and Cheryl. Leonard was Alicia and Cheryl's uncle. Henry would invite the whole family by some Friday nights, and they would fry chicken and catfish, drink hard liquor, play cards, and have a grand-old time. They did this in spite of the condition of the apartment. They seemed to ignore the condition of the environment. The bathroom, the kitchen, nor the bedroom bore any semblance of cleanliness. Henry's sheets on his bed were left unwashed for weeks at a time. Dishes would pile up in the sink. In the meantime, he would be in the kitchen trying to fry chicken and catfish.

When I first saw Alicia, I liked her. I Liked her more than Cheryl, because she was older, a little more mature, and was a yellow skinned girl. She had long-black-straight hair. I thought she was attractive. I tried my best to let her know I was interested, but she never responded in kind. She had a cold way of relating to the world, as if she had been badly hurt and neglected in her life, and was disinterested in most things and people. Her mother, Benecia, didn't make it obvious in front of Henry and I, but knowing her, Alicia and Cheryl had probably been through to hell and back. At the time, I thought it was me. She demonstrated no interest in me whatsoever and was unresponsive toward me.

Benecia weighed at least three-hundred-fifty pounds, with yellow skin, and was about five-seven. Needless to say, she was a big woman. Even though she was a big woman, she was a beautiful woman.

Alicia had a thin waist with a C-cup breast. She was a 34-22-38, five-five, and weighed about one-twenty-five. She was statuesque with a doll like face. She carried herself as if she was the Queen of Sheba. She had the habit of stepping like a prize show pony.

Cheryl was much the same as Alicia, except she was darker, and one inch taller. She also had a C-cup, was about 32-22-36. She was a few years younger than Alicia. She weighed about one-twenty. She was also statuesque with a doll like face. She carried herself with even more dignity than Alicia. They were both blessed with good looks.

Even though they seemed to have such high regard for themselves, I had been around the block a few times, and could see beneath all that facade and put on. I wasn't buying their act.

One day Alicia, Cheryl, and Benecia came over. I tried to get them both to go dancing with me. Henry agreed to let me use the car.

"It's Saturday night; why don't we go dancing?" I asked.

I figured we could go dancing rather than sit around that drab apartment. Also, maybe they would open up a bit if I could get them in another setting.

"I'm not prepared to go dancing, and only came for a minute," Alicia said.

"We wouldn't have to stay that long."

"I don't really like to dance. I have two left feet, and never got into dancing," Alicia said.

"Don't worry, I can teach you."

I wanted to say, like some folks think, that all Blacks

folks can dance. They simply need a little practice. To tell the truth, most Black people can dance to some degree. With some of us the ability is more latent than with others. But Alicia was convinced that she had two left feet. I'm not sure what experiences she had made her feel that way.

"Some other time under different conditions," Alicia said.

It seems that Alicia was doing all the talking. I didn't intend to take no for an answer, but I had to eventually take the no. They acted as if their mother was their armor and their protection, and they were afraid to leave her. They didn't seem to feel comfortable without her. I have observed parents who fostered in their children a sense of dependency on them from an early age.

"OK, I'll take a raincheck," I said that, but at the time new I was getting ready to move on and wouldn't be around much longer.

We never got the opportunity to follow up on that raincheck for dancing. Henry went in the kitchen and started cooking some hotdogs, hamburgers, and fries. When they left, after eating, Henry called me aside.

I found out that Alicia and Cheryl didn't like school. Alicia dropped out as a junior and had been trying unsuccessfully to find a job ever since. Cheryl dropped out as a freshman. They both gave the flimsy excuse that the other girls despised them for some reason, wanted to fight them, and they both got tired of the hassle. Neither one of them sounded like someone I wanted to hook up with. Both of them only sat around every day and looked at soap operas. I like women who were not only classy but ambitious as well. I didn't want to be associated with high school dropouts. There was already enough of that in my family.

"Don't you like Alicia and Cheryl?" Henry asked.

"Yeah, I like them."

"They're some pretty girls."

"Yes, they are, but I can't get them to show any interest."

"That's just the way they are. You have to be aggressive. Benecia is the same way; they've been conditioned to expect you to show all the interest."

"Maybe I'm not aggressive enough."

Even though these girls were pretty, there was something lacking about them, they didn't seem to have much class about themselves, even though they were great pretenders. They seemed to have been afraid to open their mouths for fear someone would figure out what they were really like. Though, you couldn't ask for more beautiful girls.

"You haven't turned punk on me have you little brother?"

"What makes you ask that?"

"Because you want try to advance on two perfectly beautiful girls."

"It takes more than just being pretty."

"What does it take?"

"A good attitude."

"OK, I guess I'm viewing the situation wrong. You know what you like. I'll let you decide what you like from now on."

Henry backed down from asserting his views, but I knew his perspective really hadn't changed, and he thought I wasn't being man enough.

"Thank you! I would appreciate that."

Henry never mentioned the girls again.

I'm not sure why they eventually quit coming over. Henry told me Cheryl got pregnant a few months later. The father was unknown and otherwise un-accounted for. Some believed it was the brother-in-law, but no one had enough evidence to accuse him. Others said Henry had something to do with it, but of course he denied it. I assumed they quit coming over because of something that went on between Henry and Benecia.

I wanted to better my condition, and moved to one of the local college campuses, and entered school. It was the most positive move I knew to make at the time. I had to get away from Henry and knew living with him was only temporary. I never saw Alicia and Cheryl again, but often thought of them. I moved on with my life and never actually, to this day, saw Henry again. I'm not sure what happened to Henry. No one in the family knows if he is living or dead. He had such a liking for fried chicken, fried catfish, polish sausage, pizza, and by-products from the pig, that he has probably passed on. He had done a lot to help me during my youth. He had planted a seed, and it was time for me to make it on my own. My sister told me at my mother's funeral in 1989 that they did everything possible to find him, but no luck.

I attended two different graduate schools, got married, moved to Chicago, and never looked back.

> *"Your past will greatly influence your future,
> but don't let it determine your future."*
>
> *"Good character is the best
> characteristic one can possess."*

SEVEN

Mrs. Drexel

I actually had a poor background in English as in most subjects. Few people in my background were concerned about my education. I had to survive mostly on my internal motivation. Several people here and there helped me to survive. I don't remember having very much English in elementary, junior high, or high school. My memory of elementary school is vague, but I can't remember any serious discussions of grammar or syntax. Junior high was spent horseplaying and wasting time. Much of our time in high school was spent as downtime. I had four years of English in high school, but I can't remember a great deal about it. In college I had the regular freshman and sophomore English. No special effort was made on developing my writing skills or writing papers. My parents nor teachers were very strong on English grammar or syntax. My parents' education wasn't good enough to instruct me on the finer points of grammar or syntax. My mother only finished the eighth grade, and my father dropped out in second grade to help his family with the farm. Also, the people in my community didn't put much emphasis on English or any other aspect of education. We were a working-poor community. I should have spent more time studying English. As a matter of fact, I should have spent more time on all my subjects. I do realize that elementary school is the main place to focus on learning grammar and syntax.

I spent too much of my actual time doing chores on the farm: cutting grass, cutting wood, herding and feeding animals, and cultivating and harvesting. The rest of the time during growing season was spent plowing in the fields. If my mother caught me reading, she would quickly redirect me to other activities. After doing chores, I was usually too tired to read.

I also realized at a later point in my life, much too late, that language arts were one of my strong points. And if I had been more aware of this fact, I could have taken the time to develop in those areas. We barely had the basics: reading, writing, and arithmetic. We didn't even have the fundamentals of music, art, physical education, or speech. And I had no counsel throughout my education, and therefore drifted along, like a ship without rudder, taking the path of least resistance, and moving toward my own destruction. We often think about such things, after the fact, what we could have or should have done in such situations.

I actually had the following experience in high school. I was a freshman in high school, and finally realized that my English was substandard. My best subject was math, because we had a good math teacher, and she put forth maximum effort and energy. I don't remember any other teacher exerting that kind of effort.

What made me realize my English had been neglected was a substitute teacher asked the class a question one day. We had two classes in freshmen English. One, I considered to not have any promise, and the other had much more promise. I happened to be in the one that had no promise.

The teacher asked the class, "What's a verb?"

I raised my hand high in the air, as if I had all the information. As neglected as my background was, I still considered myself to be intelligent. I just didn't know how much I didn't know. I was in fact an ignorant young man.

"What's a verb, Charlie."

"A verb is an action word," I said.

I had heard that statement in one of my classes, from where I didn't remember.

"Give me an example," she said.

"Fast," I said.

I thought for certain that fast implied action.

"Fast is an adverb, Charlie," she said, "but sometimes depending on how it's used."

We usually attempted no serious study of the English language. We simply sat and stared out the window, at least that's what I did with most of my time. Here I was a freshman in high school and had never given serious consideration to the parts of speech. I vowed at that point to make an effort to improve my English.

After class the substitute teacher called me to the side, "What's wrong Charlie? I considered you to be one of the best students in the class."

"Sorry I let you down, Mrs. Compton."

We both looked as if we were looking far away, searching for an answer.

"Why don't you find some basic English textbooks and begin to study on your own. That's what I recommend. Sometimes you can't depend on the school. If seems that your education has been badly neglected, because I know an intelligent student such as yourself should understand at least the parts of speech."

Here I was drifting along depending on only what the teachers offered me.

"You're probably right, Mrs. Compton."

"Do you have any English books in your home?"

"No books in my home except the Bible."

"You need to get your hands on some books, and read more in general, but especially English books."

"What books do you recommend, Mrs. Compton?"

"How will you get books? There are no accessible libraries or bookstores in the area."

"My brother-in-law is a teacher in Dallas. He can probably get some books for me."

I was serious about following her suggestions and doing what it took to improve my education.

"Start off with the basic English textbook by Warriner, then read some general novels, and read any of the books on basic punctuation and grammar. In looking at your writing in general, I believe you have the potential to be a writer. You write with such clarity and imagination. When you read those, don't stop, that will be just a beginning."

I thanked Mrs. Compton for giving me the advice, and when I got a chance, I called my brother-in-law. I told him my predicament and told him what I needed.

He said he always wondered what kind of education I was getting, and that he had some basic education textbooks as well as some books on English grammar and syntax that were sitting around in his library gathering dust. These he wouldn't have to buy. At one time he taught GED classes, and used a lot of these books for that purpose. These were the first of many books he sent me.

By the end of the week he sent me 20 books. He said they would improve my English and my general education if I read them. This was the beginning of my personal and private education.

I was generally busy on the farm during planting and growing season, but most other times you could find me studying. Every night when I came in from the field, I would get deep into my books. During wintertime, on those cold nights, I would warm my heart by reading a good book. I didn't go to bed on most nights until one or two o'clock in the morning, every night during the school year. My mother would have to come in my room and insists that I go to bed.

Because of my experiences, I suppose that's why I had the following dream on a Friday night laying in my bed in a South Suburb of Chicago. This was much after my career had ended. I drifted off to sleep and found myself back in high school in that small town in East Texas.

Starting with the day Mrs. Compton informed me of my deficiencies, I read every English book I could get my hands on. We got a new English teacher my sophomore year. In the meantime, I kept my thoughts to myself. Nobody knew I was reading as much as I could. I never said much in class, but on my examinations, I made close to the highest score.

I had always been a little nervous. Mrs. Drexel didn't know anything about me and hadn't bothered to ask anyone. One day after class she called me to the side.

"How come you're so nervous? you don't have anything to be nervous about? Just relax and take your time. Things work out better that way. You seem like an intelligent young man. I can tell by your test scores and the way you respond in class."

"I'm naturally a little nervous, always have been since I can remember."

"Do you plan to attend college?" she asked.

"At this point I don't know; it may be necessary for me to get a job. My parents are having a hard time. My father is disabled, and my mother has never worked.

"You can help them better if you attend college."

"OK, I'll think about it."

Mrs. Drexel helped me with my weaknesses and fortified my strengths. When it came time for college, I was ready.

We had a writing contest held in a nearby town, and I won the contest. No one knew what was going on with me, why I was all of a sudden excelling in English. I accomplished this in view of the fact there were no accessible libraries or bookstores in any of the small towns in the area.

I did graduate and went on to college. No one expected that of me. They assumed I would get a job in one of the local factories. I made a decent score on the ACT and was accepted into the college for which I had applied. I only applied to one college, because I was sure that's where I wanted to attend. I don't know what would have happened had I not been accepted to the one college I applied. Mrs. Drexel, my English teacher made sure I got a four-year scholarship.

I did well at college, majoring in English. After moving forward with my college career for several years, in my senior year, my favorite college teacher spoke to me one day after class, "Charlie are you interested in a creative writing program?"

"I was mainly focusing on getting a job. My parents need as much help as they can get,"

"What kind of job are you interested in?"

"Anything to do with writing."

"I thought you were interested in finding a job in writing. I could tell that by the last story you wrote. You could benefit your career by attending a creative writing program."

"You think so, sir?"

"You can earn much more money and be a better help to your parents after graduating from a creative writing program."

"What program are you talking about?"

"It's the creative writing program at the University of Iowa. I can help you to get a full scholarship. It's one of the best programs in the country of its kind. If you are strapped for cash, I can also help you get a graduate assistantship. It will put some cash in your pocket for incidentals."

"You make it hard to refuse, sir."

It was February in my senior year. I told him I would let him know within several days. I thought about it, and thought about it, and considered what the writing program could do for my career.

The next time I saw Mr. Thompson, I said, "Hook me up with that Program. I believe I want to attend."

I graduated from college with a 3.5 average on a 4.0 system. Come graduation time he purchased my ticket to Iowa. Without him I don't know what I would have done. I was thankful to have such a concerned individual along the way. I kept in contact with Mr. Thompson, and he was later instrumental in helping me to get several articles and a book published.

After college I entered the creating writing program at the University of Iowa. He got me a scholarship to attend the program.

On one trip home, I visited Mrs. Compton. We talked about old times. She said she had retired. She told me about the progress of some of my fellow high school students. I told her about my progress in the writing program. She said she never expected me to get that far. But she realized that she was instrumental in planting the seed that helped me to grow and develop academically. I don't know what I would have done had she not made me aware of my potentials and possibilities. She also told me that things had changed a great deal in that small town where I went to school. The school had become so popular that students from miles around were trying to attend—even as far away as the next town.

I also visited Mrs. Drexel. She had helped me a great

deal in high school. She even helped me to complete my college application and got me that scholarship. I did become less anxious as a result of her advice. She had also retired. She wished me much luck with my career and said I would probably get much further with my career than she had ever gotten with hers. She said she was proud of me and gave me a big hug.

I then visited with Mr. Thompson, we had kept contact since college, and during the writing program. I thanked him for all his help. He was also retired, and still living in that small college town where I went to college. We got caught up on things that went on at the college and things that went on in general. I'm not sure what direction my life would have taken had he not gotten me that scholarship to the writing program.

I gave all of them my address at the University of Iowa. To my surprise, they all sent me some serious, hard, cold cash. All of them sent me at least $500.00. I never expected them to do this. They said it was a gift to help me out in my career. At this time, I badly needed some cash, it was just enough to help me finish up the program and move me to my next destination. It is true, the Almighty God will come through exactly when you need Him. I wrote them all a letter thanking them for being so kind. Before I graduated from the writer's program all my mentors had passed away.

I completed the program with honors. I graduated and began my writing career as an associate editor at a magazine. Several years later I had written several books, two of them had spent two weeks on the *New York Times* best seller's list.

In the end, all my hard work, time, effort, and energy had paid off.

Then I woke up to find it was all only a dream.

For some reason, I lie there thinking about what I should have done in my career. But it was too late for wish I should haves or could haves. They say, in any regard, hindsight is always 20/20.

> "Peace of mind is the only thing
> of value on this planet."
>
> "We try to pattern too much of our lives
> after fairytales and folktales, causing us
> to live a make-believe existence."

EIGHT

Fantasy

I was in my study one warm spring night in May 2015, in a South Suburb of Chicago. I was surrounded by my books. The books were wall to wall. I was sitting in my plush La-Z-Boy recliner while watching a rerun of "Good Times" on TVOne. I had been to a high school graduation party earlier that evening for the daughter of one of my friends (the daughter had received a free ride to Harvard), and he was celebrating; and they had plenty of ribs, polish sausage, bratwurst, pizza, fried chicken, hamburgers; and plenty of hard liquor, beer, and wine to drink. I had my fill of all that was available—and probably over did it. After I got home, I had drifted off to sleep and began to dream.

It's not uncommon for children to have dreams about and sometimes think that their parents are not their biological parents. Sometimes this is only a wish. At other times children fixate on someone they think might be a more desirable parent. The most amazing thing about this situation is that sometimes children are right. Most children have a feel for who their real parents are. It's like a calf will be able to pick out its mother, soon after being born, from among a host of potential mothers.

I hadn't thought much on the subject of incest. It seems like such a dirty word. The first time I came in contact with the subject was while reading a book about some so-called hillbillies. I don't remember the name of the particular book, just a book I came across somewhere. I am relatively sure it was a trashy fictional novel. The book suggested that this practice was common among hillbillies. Because many of them lead isolated lives, were mostly uneducated, had their own customs, and live in the hills, sometimes they acquired strange customs. I never knew if this depiction was true or if the general public is prejudiced against hillbillies. I have more than once since that time heard this custom attributed to hillbillies. Of course, incest occurs among some of the finest families in the country, and is not just peculiar to hillbillies or any other class of individuals. I always considered that anyone engaging in incest must be a degenerate of the worst kind.

We lived in a rural area at least twenty miles from a city in either direction. Consequently, I would say we were extremely isolated. Even the highway that the trail led to was curvaceous, hill-ridden, winding, and meandering. We only occasionally interacted with other people. My father/grandfather was somewhat gregarious, but my mother/grandmother believed in staying away from other people. We minded our own business, stayed to ourselves, and had our own way of doing things. About the only mainstream thing we did was to celebrate Christmas and Thanksgiving. A lot of mainstream customs we didn't adhere to.

My parents/grandparents were somewhat ignorant, and didn't realize what was necessary to raise children in the twentieth century. They didn't know how to teach their children the more correct mainstream values. They were settled in the old-fashioned ways. My parents/ grandparents saw the development of many modern inventions, yet they never changed their mind-set. They also saw many changes in society. They were both born in 1900s, and saw World War I, World War II, and the Depression come and go. Subsequently, being out of touch, some incest began to developed in our family. My mother/grandmother graduated the eighth grade (there were no local high schools), and my father/grandfather dropped out of second grade to help on his family's farm. My sister/mother also dropped out early in her education, as did my brother/father. You could say they were basically uneducated and into their own world.

My parents/grandparents brought children into

the world that they weren't prepared to deal with and care for. There were ten of us. My oldest brother/father raped my sister/mother repeatedly. I say rape, some of their encounters could have been consensual. You know how children are when they lack proper training: they sometimes respond like animals. That's how I came to exist. She was afraid to reveal the incest to my parents/grandparents. My brother/father told her he would kill her if she told. Before long I was born. My sister/mother didn't tell her parents until a month before I was born, who was the real father. Therefore, ruling out the possibility of an abortion. She had told them her boyfriend had gotten her pregnant.

On the day I was born, my brother/father said, "Take him into the woods and smash his head against a tree or against a rock. He will never be right under the conditions in which he was born." He seemed to have a lot of insight for a devious perpetrator. Because of what they had always heard about children from an incestuous relationship, they felt that I would be abnormal in some ways. He wanted to do me like some of the Native American Indian tribes, when they gave birth to a child they thought might be abnormal. Not only did the Native American Indians do this, but some other cultures (some primitive, some not so primitive) did it as well. Some will do the same to a baby if it is not a boy. Some cultures are prejudice against girl babies; they feel boys can make more of a positive contribution to their society. They thought I would have a severe handicap. The basis of the taboo against incest is the juxtaposition of many of the same genes, and thus might tend to overly display or exacerbate any negative genes. There is too much of a chance for the recessive genes to combine.

My mother/grandmother was also looking for a reason to disqualify me from life, "My, isn't he dark," that's all she could say.

My mother/grandmother was one of those who were prejudice against darker skinned people. If they could have found a legitimate reason, they might have gone along with my brother/father and disqualified me for life.

Some Black people in those days looked negatively upon their children being exceptionally dark. Being dark was all they could detect about my physical being, and they accepted me. I must have passed the minimal standards test. My brother/father was disappointed they didn't kill me. He was feeling guilty for what he had done, and thus wanted to destroy the evidence. Even many years later, when I was around him, I could see some regret in his eyes that they let me live.

My sister/mother was so ashamed that she hibernated during the time of the pregnancy. And my mother/grandmother rarely ever made an appearance in the community. Nobody in the community had any knowledge of either of them being pregnant. All they had were midwives present during my birth. They all agreed to conspire to say my mother/grandmother was the real mother instead of my sister/mother as the real mother. It was easy for them to say my mother/grandmother was the real mother. No one knew any difference between who was the real mother.

They didn't find out until time for speech development that I would have a severe stuttering problem without some help from a speech pathologist. This stuttering problem was believed to be caused by extreme isolation and no one to talk to or socialize with. We didn't get a graded-dirt road to our house until I was six years of age, and few people in the family wasted time talking to me. I had no playmates before I started school. Relatives and other family rarely visited.

One Christmas when I was four-years old, my brother/father and sister/mother responsible for my birth came home. By this time, they both had gotten married and moved away. My sister/mother lived in Dallas, and my brother/father lived on the Gulf Coast. I was walking around in pigtails, a dress, and in my bare feet, looking generally pitiful and neglected. I think my brother/father felt sorry for me and also guilty. He couldn't bare the sight of me because of his guilt.

My brother/father and sister/mother got into an argument. At the time I didn't know what the argument was about. I didn't hear any of the communication. They had been walking through one of the many trails in the community, visiting a neighbor, and became upset with one another. My other brothers/uncles and sisters/aunts were also visiting at the time. One of my brother/uncles told them that they shouldn't argue and got them to tone it down.

They postponed the argument until they got home, and it then started up again. They argued for a while, then all I saw was my brother/father walked into the room and pulled out a razor-sharp pocketknife, and he kept a .38 Special in his pocket. That testified as to his mental stability. She was lucky he didn't shoot her.

He tried to cut her in the jugular vein. My mother/grandmother quickly threw her fat arm, the size of a fence post, around her neck. It's the only thing that saved her that day. It would have been hard getting her to a hospital, with no road to our house. My mother blocked the knife with her arm from cutting my sister/mother in the neck. My mother/grandmother had to get 20 stitches in her arm the next day. If my sister/mother had been cut in the neck, there is no way she would have survived. My family would have had to hitch up a wagon and take her through the trail to the main highway. By the time they got the wagon hitched she would have been already dead. Even if she lived long enough to take the ride through that trail; on such an uneven and shaky ride, by the end of the trail, all the blood would have been drained from her body. Then they would have had to hitch a ride or drive her to the nearest hospital. By the time they got her to a hospital, she would have been dead on arrival (DOA). In addition, most hospitals were reluctant to admit and treat Black clients, and probably would have hesitated to treat her. All this would have made for a bad situation.

Much later in my life, I found out they were fighting over me. Another sister said the conversation was as follows.

"You need to take that boy back with you to the city where he can become a civilized human being," my brother/father said, "can't you see how he's growing up."

"He'll be all right. We survived," my sister/mother said.

"Sure, look at us. We almost didn't make it! It took a definite toll on us."

"He'll be all right. The farm will be good for him. I have a husband and another son to be concerned with."

"Sure, you have always been selfish, all you think about is yourself."

"Just like you, brother."

My brother/father was trying to tell my sister/mother to take me out of those woods and take me where I would grow up and have a chance of being civilized. But she wasn't hearing it. She said I would be all right on the farm, in fact, things would be better for me there. That she had a new family she was responsible for. My brother/father was apparently serious and continued his appeal to her.

"But he needs speech therapy," he said.

"Can't he find a speech therapist around here?" she asked.

"Be realistic, in these woods. There are no speech therapists in Marshall or Longview," he said. "And even if there were speech therapists, how would he get through that trail every day, and go to see one of them."

My brother/father had apparently learned something after being away from home on the coast.

"No, I don't think my husband would accept him. My husband and I have worked too hard and long in building our relationship to ruin it at this point."

"You should reconsider, that boy needs a better situation."

"Why don't you take him to live with you?"

"You know my wife and general situation. My wife works every day, and there's no one to properly look after him."

"If you thought about it long and hard enough you would figure something out, that's what you're asking me to do."

My brother/father apparently wasn't through with the argument, but my sister had made up her mind. Apparently, he had thought he could force her to re-think the issue. After the incident, everyone soon forgot about me and went their own way. My brother/father went back to the Gulf Coast, and my sister/mother back to Dallas. My brother/father continued to talk to her about taking me to the city for years, but her mind was made up. My other sisters/aunts and brother/uncles had issues of their own. In addition to other problems, there was mental illness, alcoholism, philandering, etc. The only plausible place for me to live was with my parents/ grandparents. So, I buckled up for an unsteady ride.

I stayed and grew up on the farm. Spending most of my time taking care of farm chores. I never had toys to play with, and never played games like most normal children. Before school I didn't learn my numbers, letters, colors, or geometric shapes. Along with my lack of development and my speech, I must have seemed retarded. We were so isolated that I didn't spend much time around other children or adults, and my family still didn't spend much time with me. I was left to roam the hills with the other domesticated animals.

The other children knew I was the product of incest (it somehow penetrated the community, even though they tried to keep it quiet), they took it out on my hide, and in many other ways, although they never said anything specifically to me about it. I was determined; I didn't let the other children's attitudes bother me. And I did OK in school comparatively speaking, even though I started out behind the eight ball.

My sister/mother's husband died when I was sixteen. Soon she remarried. She already had one son, she then remarried and had another. She still didn't have enough accommodations for me. My brother/father died a few years later from cancer.

Eventually I grew up and went away to college and became a successful writer. I was now living in a North West Suburb of Washington, DC, with three sons and a wife of my own.

My parents/grandparents died in 1988 and 1989 respectively. I was left to make it on my own. It was about time for me to make it on my own.

I awakened to find myself sitting in my La-Z-Boy, my son just returning from one of his forays on the town, and my wife with her hand on my shoulder, informing me it was time to go to bed. Everything was normal. I got up, had myself a glass of wine, and went to bed. Sleep always came easier after a glass of wine. I was thankful it was only a dream.

> *"Some of the best moments in your life will come immediately after storms, tribulations, trials, wars, and generally difficult times."*
>
> *"Nothing is promised to you besides some good and bad times on earth, and your ultimate death."*

NINE

Flight 1313

I was raised and attended elementary, junior high, and high school in a small-rural town in East Texas. Attended college not far away in East Texas, and then went to the military. After the military I attended two different graduate schools in Houston. After graduate school, I moved to a South Suburb of Chicago from Houston in 1974, and have made Chicago my home from 1974 until the present. I can count the number of times I have gone back to East Texas on one hand since moving to Chicago. But I somehow later decided I wanted to return to East Texas to live. They say life consists of cycles, and everyone makes a complete cycle. In moving back to East Texas, I was considering making sort of a complete cycle in my life. I somehow wanted physical proximity, and to be able to give something back to that community from which I came. To give something back and help those who might have difficulty breaking into the system—especially the young people. I believed everyone should give something back to the community that produced them. The community from which we come is usually responsible for us being who we are. We all owe something to our original community.

I had some negative memories of East Texas for a long time. Mainly of hard work, the inadequate school, plowing a mule from sunup to sunset, rats running through the walls of our house, the extremely hot weather, rain penetrating the roof of the rusty-tin-roof shack, and the difficulties of getting from one place to another. In East Texas we lived on an isolated-rural farm. There was nothing but a three-mile trail to our house until I was six years of age. When we finally got the road, we did get electricity. Mostly the only energy we used was wood for the fireplace and the stove.

My mother always wanted some of her children to continue her farm legacy. She never verbalized this to me, but I interpolated it from her behavior. I wanted to continue her legacy in a different way: by staying close to the area and staying close to the land. When I was growing up, I didn't like the area, but since living in Chicago, I had come to appreciate it more than I did at one time.

They have made a lot of progress in the area over the years: they have blacktopped and widened the road, pumped in city water, made telephone services available, acquired natural gas, improved the school system, and gotten access to the Internet. They have all the modern conveniences. A lot of people have moved back to the area. There is plenty of good hunting and fishing. It is a better place to live. Some of my classmates have never left the area, have bought land and built ranches, and are doing well for themselves.

I have just about quit flying in my older age. I have never traveled much by air in my life. During my younger years, I did do some travel by plane. But if I hadn't done much flying, this flight would certainly have done the trick to keep me from further travel.

I dreamed I went home to East Texas on some business. I was mainly trying to find a parcel of land on which to build my dream home. I had always wanted to return to East Texas and build a two-story log cabin, with a big porch surrounding the entire house. My wife wanted that surrounding porch. We have some family property, but I didn't like the location of the family property and chose to buy some personal property. The family property was too far in the backwoods. I found the perfect piece of land to build on. It was fifteen acres, with a decent size fishing pond on the property, and grounds for hunting. The things I enjoyed about East Texas was fishing and hunting as a youth. My friend and I would roam the countryside hunting and fishing. We were young, wild, and free—happy to be energetic young bucks without a care in the world. The property was even located on a high knoll in case of flooding. It was right off the main highway. It took me several days to secure the property, but the seller and I finally arrived at a meeting of the minds. I was able to get the acreage at an inexpensive rate. Since my childhood, I had been admiring this particular parcel of land, and I was surprised no one had purchased it. The land had belonged to one particular family for many years and had simply sat there and become overgrown with vegetation. I negotiated the price down to exactly what I wanted to pay. I put a down payment on the property and was headed back to Chicago. I was speeding trying to avoid missing my flight at 8:00 p.m. out of Dallas/Ft. Worth, delighted at the deal I had made, secretly thinking I had gotten away with a steal.

I was in such a hurry that I wasn't paying much attention. Somewhere between Lawrence, Texas and Mesquite, Texas, a state trooper pulled me over. I had always been leery of state troopers in small towns.

A state trooper turned on his siren, got behind me, and stopped me, "Where are you headed?" he asked.

"To catch a flight out of Dallas/Ft. Worth. I'm running late. Without applying the speed, I will miss my flight."

"Let me see your driver's license. Do you realize you're doing seventy-five m/p/h in a sixty-mile zone?"

I went into my wallet and pulled out a Chicago driver's license.

He went back to his car to check my registration, took a few minutes, and came back. I was beginning to get worried.

Before he said anything else, I told him, "This is a rental car."

"I can see that," he said.

"I just wanted to be sure you realized it and didn't think it was stolen."

He said, "There is a lot of traffic on the highway. Several accidents up and down the highway. Slow it down. The life you save may be your own. I'm only giving you a warning this time. I just wanted to be sure there was nothing wrong."

"Thank you, sir, sorry about the excess speed. I'll be certain to slow it down."

"Take it easy, now."

With that we both pulled off. I slowed down but still was able to make good time. I rushed through the airport like O. J. Simpson in his Hertz commercials. I was able to catch the flight out of Dallas/Ft. Worth at 8:00 p.m. headed for Chicago. On the flight back, Americana Airlines, Flight 1313, I ran into more than a few problems.

I didn't know the plane was overbooked until I got out of my seat to use the bathroom. I never noticed the extra passenger lounging around on the plane. A passenger came out of nowhere and took my seat while I was in the bathroom. It was of course a deception; a passenger was waiting until some weary traveler went to the bathroom so he could take over the seat. He felt he had a right to the seat as much as anyone, since the plane was overbooked. I thought the airline had rules against someone simply taking over your seat, and that when you were assigned a seat it was yours for the duration of the flight. It was a rather small plane, but I took the time to admire a fellow passenger's artwork before I went back to my seat. The seatbelt sign was off, and we could walk about the cabin. His drawings had such great structure, depth, details, and the lines were perfect. I wanted immediately to purchase some of his drawings.

I wanted to know, did he go to art school or was he just a natural talent.

"Where did you go to art school?"

"I spent two years at the Art Institute of Chicago. Some of it is natural talent."

"I have a young cousin who is a good artist and can draw especially well. Do you recommend the Art Institute as a place to study art?"

Art talent was common in most members of my family, but I didn't get any of it. I had a brother and a sister who were good at art. Unfortunately, they never had an opportunity to develop their talent.

"Yes, I would. It is an excellent place to study art."

"Do you live in Chicago and can I have your address or place of business?"

"Yes, I live in Chicago," he gave me a business card.

"Thank you, I'll discuss the school with my cousin," and I moved on.

My intuition told me not to buy any drawings, even though he was trying to sell them. I decided to visit him at his place of business later instead of making a purchase at this time. I didn't have any way to carry drawings and thought it may be awkward trying to carry them off the plane. It may have seemed unusual for someone trying to sell drawings on a commercial flight, but it didn't seem so unusual in my dream.

When I got back to my seat the cabin was full. Everyone laughed.

"Is there another seat," I asked.

The guy who took my seat said, "When you move you lose," as if it was some sort of game.

I looked at him with much contempt but didn't say anything further. I didn't want to get into a physical altercation over the seat. I really wanted to grab and strangled him or hit him and knock him completely out of my seat. I realized that it was up to the attendants to get my seat back. I always tried to avoid physical altercations when I could. Fighting would only add confusion to the situation.

"Sure, there's one more," one passenger said. "It's in the back."

I didn't pick up on the fact that the passenger was referring to the toilet seat. I picked up on that later on. The other passenger seemed to have been taking sides with the guy who took my seat against me.

I went to the back but couldn't find a seat. I figured the other passenger had only tried to further divert me from my seat. I was standing near the restroom. Suddenly the plane went upside down, the door to the restroom flew open, and some of the chemicals from the toilet splashed on my face. It was then that I understood what the passenger meant by there was one more seat. The airline knew they had overbooked and was trying to get away with it. We had almost made it and was only a short distance from landing.

I moved away from the restroom into the seating area. I was standing there for just a minute, and the plane did another upside-down maneuver. The coins in my pocket fell to the floor. The plane straightened up, and I was trying to collect my money from the floor and under one of the seats. All of a sudden, as soon as I had collected my change, the plane dipped about five feet. This happened while I was standing in the isle without a seatbelt. The captain came over the intercom and said there was a storm over the Chicago area, and to be prepared for turbulence. He said everyone must find a seat. The attendants found me a seat, and each of them found a seat themselves.

When we straighten out, we then ran into some air

currents with shifting winds and lightning. The plane started to jerk and rumble. One young lady began to confess, "Holy Father bless me for I have sinned...." Before she could finish her confession, the plane dipped another 20 ft. There was an incredible odor of burnt rubber in the cabin.

I was so shaken that it brought up what I had for lunch. One of the attendants put a towel over the mess to cover it up. I apologized, but the attendant assured me it was not my fault. She said the plane had run into some unexpected turbulence, and there was nothing anyone could do about it. She told me to sit down and relax. After I did so, I felt better. Things finally settled down, and the turbulence subsided. At least the attendants had a positive attitude.

One engine was still smoking, and the pilot shut it down, you could see the smoke from the window. Some smoke was coming into the cabin. The captain said to put on your oxygen mask to avoid any negative effects from the smoke.

As soon as things settled down a bit more, there was a rumor on the plane that there was a poisonous snake lose in the cabin, and that it had escaped from the overhead compartment. Women were standing up in their seats. There was screaming and yelling. The captain called for calm and a return to normalcy. One man located a baby boa constrictor, picked it up, and placed it back in its container in the overhead compartment. Everyone became more comfortable with the situation. Somehow this all seemed normal. The people in the cabin became more relaxed.

How much disturbance can one man stand? yet, I stood it, and put my feelings aside for that day, time, and place.

Finally, we ran into clear skies, and things settled down a bit. The captain turned on the no smoking and fasten seatbelts sign, and announced that we were over Chicago, and would be landing in approximately five minutes. He told the attendants to prepare for landing. The attendants were aware of the overbooking problem and agreed to get me reimbursement for the flight. We soon landed, and I got my things from the overhead compartment.

I never inquired why they had an overbooking problem. I indeed felt lucky to be alive. I got my luggage from the luggage area and was on my way. I probably had grounds for a suit against the airlines for overbooking the flight. Since I was alive, I counted my blessings. My wife and son picked me up at the airport.

Within a month I went back to East Texas and finished paying for the property. I had soon built that log cabin, complete with the surrounding porch, and eventually moved back to East Texas to live on a permanent basis. Life was much different than what I had known while living in the area as a youth. A lot of my anxiety about moving back had proved to be unfounded. It proves that you can go back home, under even better conditions than what you knew years ago.

I soon woke up even though I had an exceptionally hard time doing so. I awakened in my warm-comfortable bed in Butterfield Place, a subdivision in a South Suburb of Chicago.

TEN

Math Scandal

I lived in the small town called Hallsville in East Texas. A town of approximately 1,300 in 1966. We lived in a rural area, about twenty miles southeast of the town. Hallsville was ten miles north of Marshall and ten miles south of Longview. As you can imagine the town only had a post office, a bank, two gas stations, several general stores, a Dairy Queen, and a café. Dallas was only 125 miles to the north. There were no libraries in the area that we had access to and no bookstores. The school had approximately 500 students. It was one of those old-fashioned schools that had an elementary, junior high, and high school in the same physical location. It had existed for many years without change. As far as I know, for most of that time, we had had the same principal. Recently, we had gotten a new principal. Because we had the same principal for so long was probably part of the reason the school hadn't progressed as it should have.

We had only the Three-R's: math, English, history, science, typing, and shop. We had only a minimal in our curriculum. My parents never encouraged me to get an education, and I wasn't aware enough to seek an education on my own. For a long time, the school didn't have a library, we finally got a makeshift library in high school, but it was furnished with books discarded from the larger school district. For some reason, the library soon became defunct. I'm not sure if the students walked away with the books or what happened.

I wasn't seriously challenged in anything but math. The other classes were just a matter of going through the motions. We usually only sat there with nothing but downtime on our hands. No one, to my knowledge, ever questioned the fact that we wasted so much time. The school tended to also put a lot of emphasis on shop, and few of us were going to be farmers or participate in an agricultural economy. In my freshman year we spent half the day in shop. We could have been studying something much more beneficial for our development. I need-ed speech therapy, but there was none available for me. I can think of a number of students who could have benefited from speech pathology.

In math we had Basic Math, Algebra I, Geometry, and Algebra II. The math teacher was excellent, and she did the best she could. She taught basics first and proceeded in a logical fashion. She explained everything systematically. She never gave us anything on the test that we hadn't covered in the lecture. This was uncharacteristic of some teachers. The teacher was serious about her role.

The teacher used the same tests, books, and homework assignments for several years. This gave the students a chance to accumulate a file on the teacher. The seniors got together as freshman and decided to make a file of the teacher's homework, assignments, and test. The students did that to make things easier for everyone.

By the time I was a senior, we had a full file of all the teacher's homework, tests, and assignments; with all the problems fully solved and explained. A group of students worked on this together, and there was no one student to blame for the transgression. Word got back to the teacher before long about the file the students had on her, and needless to say she was upset.

The teacher tried to find out who was responsible, but had difficulty finding out who was the culprit. She said if she found out who did it, she would have them expelled or suspended. She told the students they had two days to turn in the original and any copies of the file to her. She said no one would be punished if the files showed up mysteriously on her desk. She was able to get copies of all the files. The principal got involved, and said if he found out what seniors were involved, he would make sure they didn't graduate.

After all was said and done, the students felt bad about the situation. They knew they had badly insulted Mrs. Thompson. Mrs. Thompson was considered the best teacher we had. The only teacher who provided a rigorous and systematic approach to the subject matter. Without her we would have been missing something.

The teacher and the principal called in several students, but none of the students would admit to it. All the students had agreed not to admit to it under any circumstances. It was even more difficult for the teacher and principal to find out who specifically compiled the file, because no one knew exactly who was responsible.

I was considered one of the better math students. So, the teacher and the principal called me first into her office during her free period. The teacher and the principal had a disgruntled look on their face, as if they were completely serious.

"Ed, do you know anything about this file that was put together on Mrs. Thompson?" the principal asked.

"No, I don't know anything about it. What type of file was it?" I was trying to demonstrate complete ignorance of the whole situation.

I knew he could see right through me. Any man in his position could read me like a book. Without being able to do so, he wouldn't have gotten as far as he had.

"The file on Mrs. Thompson that contains all of her homework, tests, and assignment; with all the problems completely solved and explained."

Mrs. Thompson laughed; she knew I was playing him for all the situation was worth. We had all been advise not to admit to anything.

"I never heard of it."

"Your grades are good. You have an "A" average in math all the way through high school. Have you ever taken advantage of this so-called file?" the principal asked.

"No, I haven't, sir."

We had all been advised to burn the file in our possession, and not have any evidence of the file lying around at our homes, just in case the teacher and principal wanted to get creative and have someone check us out at home. I had taken advantage of the file since my class in geometry in my junior year. Without that file, I couldn't have maintained an "A" average, and the same goes for some of the other high-ranking students.

The principal tried to bluff, "We're going to catch the ones who are responsible for this, and everyone who is involved will be expelled or suspended, depending on the nature of their involvement. If you know anything about it, you had better admit to it now. Being a senior, if we find out later that you had any involvement, you may not be able to graduate."

I knew it was a bluff and wasn't scared. All the students vowed to stick together. I had no reason to believe that any of them would turn evidence and reveal the students' names who were involved.

The teacher said, "I'm disappointed that so many of my good students could've possibly been involved in this scheme."

"I know nothing about it, Mrs. Thompson. No way I'd do such a thing."

Knowing I was sitting right in the middle of the scandal. But I tried to keep a straight face and not reveal any weaknesses.

"If I ever find out that you were involved, Ed, I'm going to especially be disappointed in you," Mrs. Thompson said.

"Thanks for giving us your time," the principal said.

Next, they called in Harold for an interrogation. He was a senior and an excellent student. They somehow figured the seniors were mostly responsible for some reason. Someone must have fed them some type of information. Harold told me later about the interview. Again, it was the principal and Mrs. Thompson.

"Harold, do you know anything about this so-called secret file? I mean, have you ever seen such a file?"

"No, I haven't seen this file."

Harold was one of the main ones who compiled the file. But again, no one knew the exact students who put it together.

"I hear you're a great student, Harold, why would you need a file on the teacher, except to do it to help the other students?" the principal said.

"It's never been necessary for me to cheat. I've never

ran into a math problem I couldn't solve, if I put my mind to it."

"Then, have you ever even heard about such a file?"

"No, I honestly haven't, sir."

At that point they knew he was lying. By this time everybody had heard of the file. Harold later told me that he didn't believe they thought he was being honest with them.

"If we find out you had anything to do with this file, you may not be able to graduate," the principal said.

Harold said at that point he got nervous. His mother and father were teachers and planed on him attending Howard University in the fall. He made a 30 on the ACT Test; and scored high in math, reading, and social science. At this point he said they had him almost scared enough to tell the truth. The principal knew just what to say to coerce and cajole him into revealing what he knew. But he stuck to his guns, kept saying he didn't know anything about the file, in spite of his fears. He knew that if everyone kept saying they didn't know anything about it, there was nothing any of them could do.

"I understand sir."

"I personally know your parents have great plans for you, you had better tell us the truth."

Harold knew the principal was telling the truth. In fact, his father and the principal had been on Lake Bluff fishing together and had also hunted together. When the principal brought his parents into the situation, it scared him even more. But he decided no matter what the principal said, he wasn't giving in. He wasn't going to be a turncoat.

"You're right sir."

"OK, Harold, thanks for taking time to talk to us," the principal said. "Go back to your class and forget about the matter. We'll handle it."

Because of the principal's relationship with Harold's father, the principal felt a special sense of obligation for Harold's education, and under no circumstances wanted to be responsible for interrupting it.

The teacher and the principal saw they weren't getting anywhere with the higher performing seniors, so, they decided to interrogate a lower performing sophomore. Fortunately, they interviewed someone who knew absolutely nothing about the scandal. That's probably why James was a lower performing sophomore student, because he knew nothing about the easier way to do things. James was totally oblivious to what was going on with the homework, test, or assignments.

"James, have you heard about what's going on with the file?" the principal asked.

"What file? I try the best I can to mind my own business; I know nothing about a file."

At that point they realized they had chosen to interview the wrong student and changed the direction of the interview. He spoke with such honesty and confidence.

"How are you getting along in your math class?" Mrs. Thompson asked.

"I'm doing OK; I'm passing."

"Do you find yourself needing some help with your work?"

"I could use a little help."

"Next time you need some help come and see me. My office hours are posted," Mrs. Thompson told him.

"Thanks for taking time to come in," the principal said.

They saw that they were beating a dead horse in talking to James, and abruptly ended the interview.

After talking to James, they gave up on their interviews, the idea of suspending anyone, and possibly expelling anyone.

I heard the teacher and the principal gave up partially because the superintendent advised them to. The superintendent said such an incident fell within the line of normal student behavior. He said if you imposed a scheme on students, and gave them a way out, they would likely find a way to take that way out.

We were all happy to move on with our lives but had learned a valuable lesson. That is, to take your medicine just as the doctor prescribes it for you and stay away from shortcuts.

By May, it was all forgotten, about the matter of the

math scandal. The next year the school changed books, and the teacher gave different assignments, homework, and tests. From that point on the teacher varied her homework, assignments, and tests.

We all did graduate as seniors that year, and no one was expelled or suspended. We all got on with our challenge of facing the world more concretely. The students would talk about the scandal at Hallsville for years to come. Students from other schools would discuss it as well.

For some reason, I heard the math teacher decided to resign, one year later. I'm sure she would have no problem finding another job—if she didn't somehow retire. I credit her with keeping me motivated, self-assured, and interested in school. Without her I may have been just another dropout. She was one of the best teachers I have ever had. I'm glad she graced my life for the brief period of time that she did. She gave me some confidence and self-assurance in my ability as a student.

It was March of 1966. I had taken the ACT Test and made an above average score of 25. I was surprised that most of my points came from math. I received few points from social science or reading. We hadn't been encouraged to read anything but the textbooks, and we were rarely encouraged to read them.

I applied to college, partially because of the confidence and assurance I had gained in math class. I should have majored in math; it was my strongest subject. My confidence was still limited when competing with other students who had been taught trigonometry, algebra/trigonometry, and calculus in high school. I felt I couldn't compete with them on their level.

I decided to major in sociology and obtained a "B" average for my four years of work. Later I attended a graduate program in social work and guidance and counselling. I kept switching back and forth. I also studied toward a Ph.D. in sociology at two different Midwestern universities.

I saw the principal at our tenth-year high school reunion. Much later I heard Mrs. Thompson was doing well and living in Memphis, and the principal had passed away.

I believe some of the teachers expected us to give up on life, stay down home on the farm, or get a job at one of the local factories. That was the highest hopes they had for us. But we were smart enough to carry out the math scandal.

> *"When you believe you know everything, most likely you don't know much of anything."*
>
> *"Don't ignore all the warning signs, and keep right on thinking, without fact or evidence."*

ELEVEN

Superstition Ain't the Way

I was born in Hallsville, Texas, a small town in East Texas. Spending most of my time plowing a mule on a fifty-acre-dirt farm, from sunup to sunset, at the end of a three-mile trail. We were 20 miles from Marshall (45,000), 20 miles from Hallsville (1,300), 50 miles from Shreveport (200,000), 30 miles from Longview (100,000), and 150 miles from Dallas (1,000,000). For all intent and purpose, we were relatively isolated. We lived in a rusty-tin-roof shack. This shack leaked when it rained, and a strong wind could be felt indoors during the winter. It was unbearably hot during the summer.

I grew up, graduated high school, went to college, joined the Navy, was discharged from the Navy, went to graduate school, and moved to Chicago. We first lived in an apartment for two years, but soon purchased a four-bedroom brick house in one small suburban community in 1976. We later purchased a two-story, red-brick, five-bedroom house, in another small community in the South Suburbs of Chicago. We bought the house in 1998 in June. The house was on a tree-lined street in a pleasant neighborhood, and it was a nice house. There were many friendly neighbors, good-positive schools, and good shopping. It was definitely a better community than the one we moved from, and we liked the house better, it gave us more room.

I was raised in a family that believed in voodoo, witchcraft, superstition, mysticism, and religion. So, I guess I couldn't help but to pick up some of their beliefs. I didn't realize that I harbored some of these beliefs until the spring of 2019, in March. My folks believed that voodoo was responsible for what was essentially a schizophrenic condition in our family. I've read that some people who normally can't control their own destiny turn to superstition, religion, and mysticism. Some of my family members believed the voodoo lady could treat their schizophrenic condition. They didn't understand or know what schizophrenia was; nor did they understand any other abnormal mental health condition. All they could do was function from what they were aware of.

They burned candles of various types, depending on the situation, to ward off evil spirits. Sprinkled their shoes with salt, black pepper, and saltpeter. Drank vinegar. Took a bath in saltpeter. Sprinkled salt and black pepper around the house to ward off evil spirits. Kept bottles of potions hanging over the front door to the house to ward off evil spirits. They also engaged in many other rituals as well. Whenever threatened with a catastrophe, they would make a visit to see the voodoo lady, trying to find an answer to the problem.

Superstition goes back a long way in my family. My mother and some other members of the family believed that certain members of the community were trying to voodoo them. I remember my cousin brought my mother some sheets for Christmas. My mother suspected foul play and wouldn't sleep on them until she got the approval of the voodoo lady. The voodoo lady said the sheets were fixed, and for my mother to bring the sheets to her. The voodoo lady was going to undo any negative effects put on the sheets. We never heard from the sheets or the voodoo lady again.

My mother felt that a particular neighbor was trying to voodoo her and bring her family to ruin. She felt that he was putting things around the doorstep and waiting for an opportunity to put something deleterious in her well. She thought he wanted to injure her animals, burn her house and barn, and cut her fences. One cousin was a hunter, he killed more squirrels than he needed that day, and brought several to her. My mother said he had probably fixed them. My mother never left home very often for fear her enemies would have a better opportunity to hex her. The only places she went with any frequency was to town, to church, and to see the voodoo lady.

One of my sisters believed this voodoo thing was all in my mother's and other family member's minds. The sister advised me to stop eating my mother's cooking and learn to cook for myself. She said my mother had some strange ideas she had gotten from the voodoo lady and might do anything the voodoo lady said. She might even go as far as putting something deleterious in my food, trying to protect me from the hexes and spells of the neighbors. My mother was definite that the neighbors were trying to destroy her. She became definitely paranoid.

I remember my mother having a conversation with my brother, Larry. Larry had picked up some misconstrued ideas from my mother and some of the voodoo ladies they frequented. The voodoo lady gave my mother some relief from all her consternation. You could see the relief in her eyes and in her physical appearance after she visited one of them.

"The neighbors are trying to get us," my mother said.

"They can't do anything as long as we keep them at a distance," my brother said.

"I fear something is going on. The dogs wouldn't quit barking last night."

"I heard then barking also," my brother said.

"The dogs aren't going to let anyone get close to the house."

"They're slick though, they might be able to get around the dogs somehow," my brother said.

"They know exactly what to do to get you."

My mother and Larry felt the neighbors could find a way to get to them. That's why they kept going to the Voodoo lady, to ward off any hexes or spells they could place on them.

I always felt that it was difficult for anyone to do anything to you, if they couldn't put something in your food, and if they put something in your food, that was poison instead of voodoo. Poison is a physical condition, and has nothing to do with superstition, mysticism, voodoo, or the supernatural.

This belief in superstition and voodoo was a part of their schizophrenic condition. Several members of the family developed paranoid schizophrenia, and my mother resorted to the same old treatment approach: seeing the voodoo lady. I don't believe that any of them were ever helped by seeing the voodoo lady. This belief in the superstitious did stick with me for a long time, even after living in Chicago for forty years.

To my mother, she had few friends, everybody was a potential enemy trying to place a hex or spell on her. This somehow played out in the family dynamics. In that, there were no brothers or sisters, but everyone was an adversary. Even with ten children this was a very real situation. A brother or sister in my family would be more likely to cut your throat than anyone on the street; a brother or sister were more likely to take the side of a stranger. And for Heaven sakes, don't look to your brother or sister for help, because they had no allegiance to you. If one tried to live with the other until they could get a start in life—nothing going—the situation would soon erupt in a fight of some kind. Sociologists refer to such a family as a discordant family.

After growing up in that environment; since then I have studied sociology as an undergraduate; social work at the Masters' level; and studied toward a Ph.D. in sociology at two different Midwestern universities; and still haven't overcome some of the mysticism, superstition, and religious ideas implanted in my mind at the time. All of these schools certainly taught me against superstition, mysticism, religion, and magic.

This leads to the main point of my story: how I adopted this superstitious perspective, and how it played out in my situation. A robin kept fluttering and banging into our windows. This banging and fluttering would begin late at night and end early in the morning. The robin would come to the same window every day. This occurred for about a week. I don't quite see how the robin could stand the blows it was inflicting upon itself. But apparently it was designed to make and withstand the blows as a part of whatever the ritual it was engaged in. My wife had never seen a bird, or any other animal of any kind do this before. She wondered what was wrong with it. She was in great consternation as to what was wrong with it.

"Did you hear that robin last night?" she asked me.

"That's just a part of their mating ritual," I said.

Being raised around animals, I knew something of their behavior.

"That's no mating ritual, I believe there's something wrong with the bird."

"There's nothing wrong with it. It's probably his mating season."

"I don't believe it. I believe there's something wrong with it."

"What could be wrong?"

"How do you know the robin is engaging in a mating ritual," my wife asked.

"Because I know a little about animal behavior."

"You're joking with me. Most human beings don't know anything about animal behavior, and when they do, it's because they observed one particular species for years. All animal species have different practices."

"You're probably right but believe what I say."

"Have you ever seen a bird act like that before?"

"Not really, but it's a matter of logical induction and deduction. It's the only explanation. If the bird was sick, it would simply go off somewhere and die. It wouldn't be beating it's body against the window."

"You don't know that for sure."

"I'm not saying it's a fact for sure, I'm simply making a college-boy guess. But you're right, I have seen a lot of birds, but never saw one act like that before. He's not trying to get you to put food in the bird feeder, because robins eat worms, they don't eat grain. Animals can have some strange mating rituals. At least it seems that way to human beings," I said.

As soon as I got out of diapers, my mother turned me lose with the rest of the domesticated animals on the farm. I fed them, herded them, killed them. and almost lived with them. So, I know something of animal behavior. I spent a lot of time with the animals. That's how I came to the conclusion that the robin was engaging in a mating ritual.

The robin was keeping both of us up practically all night. The noise was loud, sounded like someone hitting a gong with a rubber mallet. If you looked out the window, it was so highly sensitive and alert that it would quickly fly away. When you left the window, it would then come back to the window and resume its activities as quickly as it had left. The robin seemed desperate to accomplish some objective. The bird would keep up this noise for a number of hours.

I figured it was a part of the birds mating ritual, or could it be the "angel of death" coming for someone. Being semi-superstitious, I kept thinking maybe it was the latter. I didn't want to mention such a far-out concept to my wife, but certainly such an idea was circulating in the back of my mind. I'm not sure how I got this idea in my head, but it somehow came to me to be within the realm of possibility.

The robin got on with its life in about a week, never came back to the window, but left behind a series of events that would lead one to wonder about superstition.

About a week after the robin quit going through his ritual, my aunt passed away. She died of cancer, two heart attacks, and pulmonary disease. She fell ill suddenly and had never had any major medical problems.

A weeks after that, my uncle died in a horrible traffic accident. A driver was coming down the wrong way on a one-way street. It was a head-on collision. He died instantly.

Several days later, my first cousin died in a horrible factory accident. He stepped on and uninsulated electric cable and died of electric shock.

A week after that, my brother died in a car accident. The car ran upon the sidewalk and hit him. The body was badly dismembered.

I didn't firmly believe in superstition, but it was a part of my background. I decided to have a talk with my wife about the situation anyway.

"Do you think that robin was trying to warn us about the bad news of the series of deaths from back home."

"With all your education, you're not still superstitious, are you?"

"Not really, but you should never underestimate superstition."

"I'd believe it was a mating ritual before I believed in superstitions."

"It could have been the 'angel of death' trying to warn us about what was to come."

Somewhere in my past, I'd heard something about the "angel of death," and it brought back memories.

"There is no such thing as an 'angel of death.' That's just a concept you came up with out of your superstitious background."

The robin was soon a thing of the past, and we forgot about the robin as the "angel of death." We also forgot about the robin as engaging in a mating ritual. I guess we will never know the truth of whether or not the bird was engaging in a mating ritual, unless we consult an ornithologist who specialize in studying the behavior of robins.

With all the modern technology, you would think that superstitious individuals are a thing of the past. But I assure you that they are still with us. I personally know many individuals who still believe in voodoo, mysticism, magic, the supernatural, and have some strange ideas about religion.

I know believing that the robin had something to do with these deaths is merely superstition, but it is easy to believe that it did, if you let your imagination run wild. "Superstition ain't the way."

> *"Doing what is popular can sometimes cause you to travel a difficult path."*
>
> *"Don't follow the crowd. Ninety-five percent of the time the crowd is wrong."*

TWELVE

Graduation Ghost

I was sitting in my comfortable La-Z-Boy at 12:00 midnight. It was the middle of February. We owned a two-story brick house in a South Suburb of Chicago. The temperature was 20 degrees below freezing. My wife and I had just finished watching an episode of "Perry Mason"—her favorite TV show. She tends to like lawyer and detective shows. I was tired and decided to go to bed. I had a habit of lying in bed while watching the Word Network. The Word Network contains some of my favorite programming This is a religious network that broadcast 24/7.

Usually it took me a while to fall asleep. Normally, I had to do breathing exercises in order to get to sleep. I suffered from mild insomnia. After turning from side to side, I finally went to sleep, and found myself back

121

in East Texas. I am from a small-rural town in East Texas. This town is along the Arkansas, Louisiana, and Texas border. Sometimes the area is referred to as the ARK-LA-TEX.

I was sleeping hard back in my old bed in East Texas. It was Thursday morning just before school. It was the end of May, and my bed was warm and comfortable, the sun was rising, and I resisted getting up. My mother informed me that I had better get up and get ready for school. We didn't have a bathroom, and my mother never fixed breakfast. But I kept dallying around until the bus pulled up to our house. Our house was the last stop on the red-dirt road, and we lived at the end of this road. Usually the bus driver would turn around and wait for me. It was rare if he didn't wait. If he didn't wait, I could always drive my car. I preferred to drive anyway.

He was blowing his horn to the tune of a symphony. Finally, my mother told me I had to get going. I quickly put on some short pants, some gym shoes, an old T-shirt, and grabbed my book bag—it was light because we had already turned our books in, and headed out the door. I came out just in time to get on the bus. The door was open, and he closed it and pulled off. The bus driver was about to depart.

I arrived at school at the proper time—around 8:30 a.m. However, I had difficulty finding my homeroom. I looked around for several minutes but was unable to find the room. Every room I looked in it seemed there was some other class in the room. Every room I looked in nobody paid me any attention. It was like I was a ghost. I didn't have to open the door to look in, all the rooms had big plate-glass windows. I assumed my homeroom teacher had made some other plans for the students for that day without my having paid attention to what was supposed to happen for that day.

Finally, I located the appropriate room. For some reason, I found it to be exactly where it should have been. I had looked in that room earlier, but there was no one in the room. For some reason, the students were slightly late coming to class.

Finally, all the students were present and accounted for. I was in a feisty mood that day. It was near the end of school, and seniors only had one more day. Everyone was dressed in their fineries: the boys had on their best shoes, pants, and shirts—and some had on a suit; the girls had on their best dresses, high heels, and necklaces. Many of the boys and girls had gotten expensive watches for their graduation present. Everyone either had gotten a haircut or had their hair done. I didn't know how to explain the fact that I was so poorly dressed to the rest of the class, so I got a little feisty with Helen, one of my female classmates. The only reason why I attacked her was because she was looking so good. She had on a red-mini dress, with black-silk stockings, medium-height high heel shoes, an adorable watch and necklace, and her hair was perfectly done. I didn't know at the time that for some reason she was the only one that could hear or see me. I suppose supernatural forces had picked her out to be my medium.

"What's up mama?" I asked Helen.

"I'm not your mama," replied Helen. "But I'm doing fine brother man."

I knew my behavior was odd and thought I'd attack someone before they attacked me for being so poorly dressed on senior's day.

"You and I should get together sometimes."

"Why hadn't you bothered to ask me before today? I'm leaving for Dallas as soon as I graduate. My schedule is busy until then. Besides, you've known me since first grade, and you've never shown the slightest bit of interest."

I couldn't explain my lack of interest, but most of the students were leaving for the big city of Dallas soon after graduation. Most of them were tired of rural living. We were approximately 125 miles south east of Dallas, and it was the closest mega city in the area. At least she did act as though she would have been interested had she received an earlier invitation.

"Would you really have gone out with me if I had asked you earlier in our high school career?"

"I might have. You image is not as bad as you think."

All this was said in hearing distance of the other students, and no one had looked my way, or asked why I was dressed so poorly on senior's day. Being a rebel, they probably thought I was trying to break away from what was traditional and customary for seniors. Another young man she had been close to came over and kissed her on the mouth. For some reason that angered me. I didn't realize that he could neither see or hear me, even though I was sitting right next to her, and looking directly in her eyes. I had no reason to respond the way I responded to her.

All of a sudden, I lashed out at her, "You little devil."

"What's your problem? What does my friend kissing me have to do with you?"

"You knew that you and Johnny were cozy, yet you were cozying up to me. That's why I called you a devil. I was about to ask you to the social tonight."

"Sorry, I'm going with Johnny."

The teacher said, "Listen up. All seniors will remain in their homeroom today. And be sure you pick up your cap and gown, and that you are at the graduation exercises on time Friday night and Sunday evening. Don't forget the social tonight." She spoke in a nonchalant fashion and once again left the room.

All of a sudden, I realized that I couldn't remember actually riding on the bus that morning. The last recollection I had was heading out the door on my way to the bus, but no actual memory of being on the bus. Usually some word that was said, a fight, or some other activity catches my attention or brings to mind the ride on the bus. My brother had purchased me a sharp 1963 black Chevrolet Impala, with some expensive-chrome rims, and two guns coming straight out the back. I would drive to school whenever I felt the need for a change. But I also couldn't remember driving my car.

It then came to me that I had been driving and drinking with some of my friends on Wednesday night. The last thing I remember, before this morning, was leaving the basketball game last Wednesday night with Larry and Jeff.

I figured out that something must have happened between Wednesday night and Thursday morning. My abrupt way of coming to school must have been my way of saying good-bye to my fellow students. That is if they already hadn't heard. News travels slowly in the backwoods of East Texas.

I did notice that the other students had little to say to me while I was engaged with Helen. Usually someone would tell me if I was getting out of line. Even the teacher acted as if I didn't exist.

I was sitting there thinking when all of a sudden, I finally remembered. My friends and I left the game about ten o'clock and decided to go to Longview to get some beer. Hallsville was a dry town. We were on our way on Highway 80, headed back to the Quagmire Café. The Quagmire Café was where we chilled out and got our thoughts together. We had purchased two six packs of Budweiser and were vigorously drinking it.

I wasn't paying as much attention to the road as I should have been.

Larry and Jeff both had dropped out of school the previous year and went to work at the pottery factory in Marshall. So, they had no idea what was going on in school. They used me to catch up on things. We struck up a conversation about school.

"Who're you dating at school these days?" Jeff asked me.

"I'm not dating anyone at the school but have a few girlfriends in Marshall that you probably don't know."

"All my girlfriends are in the opposite direction: Longview," Jeff said.

"Are you glad you dropped out of school and went to work?" I asked, addressing both Jeff and Larry.

"It's the best thing I could have done," Larry said. "The only thing I miss a lot is being near that fine Mrs. Johnson."

Mrs. Johnson was the social studies teacher, and she was beautiful. She had perfect legs, a perfect body, and kept herself neat and immaculate. All the male students had a crush on Mrs. Johnson.

"I was wasting my time," said Jeff, "I wasn't doing anything. I spent too much time picking cotton, and not enough time on my studies. Going out west to pick cotton until late October every year kept me behind the eight ball."

Both Jeff and Larry's families had a practice of going

out west to pick cotton from September through late October. It was a holdover from the time Blacks got time off from school to work the plantation and had a shorten school year and school day to work on the plantation. Plantation work for Blacks was more important than schoolwork. Some families, even in the 1960s, supplemented their family income by engaging their whole family in picking cotton. These families valued short-term economic gain over long-term educational gain.

Both Larry and Jeff's families encouraged them to drop out of school. They couldn't see the importance in getting an education. The boys were especially encouraged to drop out and go to work at the local factory. The girls seemed to have been encouraged to graduate high school. This had occurred in Jeff's and Larry's families for a long time. Their brothers had followed the same pattern.

"I sometimes think I should've dropped out and went to work, but I'm a senior now, and will be graduating later in the week," I said.

"It doesn't matter," Jeff Said, "you'll only be able to get the same jobs that we'll be able to get."

"He's telling the truth," Larry said.

"I'm not going to stop with high school, I'm going on to college," I said.

"Even then you may not have a better opportunity of getting a better job. The system is rigged," Jeff said.

"Give him a break," Larry said, "it's not all that bad. Some Blacks get good jobs as teachers, preachers, social workers, and a number of other professions."

"I have to admit, it may not be all that bad," Jeff said.

"But my brothers are doing OK, even though they dropped out of high school and moved to Dallas," Larry said.

"Mine too," Jeff said.

"Your earning potential is much greater if you graduate high school and go on to college," I said. "I bet they could have done a lot better if they had stayed in school."

I didn't like to preach about the benefits of an education to those who had dropped out. I figured they had their values and I had mine. It only generated more jealousy, envy, and hard feelings. I had the benefit of an older brother who regretted not finishing his education and realizing its value. This was the brother who bought me the car and saw the need to give me money and encourage me. My actual parents were worse than Jeff and Larry's when it came to encouraging me to get an education.

I detected that Larry and Jeff were a little jealous that I had stayed in school and had high hopes of going on to college. It wasn't the first times jealousy and envy had raised their ugly head in the relationship.

Most of the boys in the neighborhood usually dropped out of high school as a freshman and went to work in one of the local factories. A little more time and they would move away to Dallas.

We had drunk the last of our two six packs and were wanting for more beer.

"I told you guys we should've gotten a case rather than two six packs," Jeff said. He seemed to get angry.

"It's too late now, we're almost to Hallsville," Larry said.

"We'll have plenty of time to get more beer on another day. You guys act like they're going to run out of beer," I said.

I looked around, "Hand me another beer before the fight starts."

Just as I put my hand back for the last beer. Before I could look back around at the road.

Larry yelled out, "Look out."

Several deer suddenly crossed the road. I was traveling about sixty-five miles an hour. I hit my breaks, but the car skidded, and hit several trees. I finally remembered the car erupting in flames.

I only realized there was something wrong because that morning when my mother told me to get up and get on my way to school, I didn't see her. I only heard her voice. I also recall that it was strange that I didn't see my car parked next to the house where it usually sits. I didn't pay much attention because I was in such a hurry to get to school.

I woke up in my mahogany-wood-frame bed, with my

60" smart TV blaring the words of Mike Murdock—a well-known evangelist. I jumped out of bed just as my wife was opening the door to our bedroom. She told me to go back to sleep, and that I was probably having a bad dream. I told my wife all about the dream, but she offered no interpretation. Neither of us usually wasted time trying to interpret each other's dreams. We simply took each other's dreams as just dreams. I said to myself, "Thank God I was fortunate enough to have survive."

THIRTEEN

My Career as a Truck Driver

I graduated high school and considered myself lucky to have made that achievement. I had no thoughts of attending college, or even a trade school. I had few ambitions. I knew my education was inadequate and hadn't prepared me for mainstream competition in the work force or for life in general. I had few sufficient role models that I could emulate. I had five sisters and four brothers, only four of them graduated high school: one of my brothers and three of my sisters. The highest position held in the work force, in my immediate family, I knew about, was two of my brother-in-law's: one was an auto mechanic and the other was a teacher. They both lived in nearby cities, but I had limited contact with them.

My parents both came from poor farm families. The only job my mother ever had was to help manage that small-dirt farm; my father worked as a janitor in an oil refinery on the Gulf Coast. Prior to that he had helped to manage the farm, and did pick-up jobs when he could, to help put food on the table. All of my sisters and brothers took whatever jobs they could find. Also, we lived in a working-poor community, and people in the community generally took whatever jobs they could find.

When you went looking for a job, you always knew beggars couldn't be choosy. I had no role model except looking for whatever job I could get. My sisters and brothers had spent all their time trying to help manage that small-dirt farm we lived on and had not acquired any specific skills. I had spent from sunup to sunset ploughing and doing other chores on the farm, and had acquired no specific set of skills, except for how to manage a small-dirt farm. Even if you had skills a good job was difficult to get, and without some skills a good job was almost impossible. In addition, I had a severe stutter, was slightly nervous, and had spent more than my share of time being isolated.

I had a brother who worked construction most of his life, and a brother who drove a truck for most of his life. Both of these brothers had worked for their companies for many years. The other two had no consistent employment, did a few menial jobs, and was unemployed the majority of the time. I decided I would try for driving a truck. My brother had taught me to drive when I was eleven-years old. With a truck all you had to do was drive. I figured I could do that easily enough. I felt construction work was too hard on the body. I checked out several truck driving companies after high school. They all told me I had to be twenty-one and have a valid CDL driver's license. I decided the only thing to do was to go into the Army for four years if I indeed wanted to make a career of driving a truck. The Army would give me a chance to grow, mature, and develop. When I graduated high school, I was eighteen.

So, I joined the Army and spent four years. I didn't want to make a career out of the Army, just stay long enough to turn twenty-one, so I could get a CDL license and drive trucks. This would give me some time to get it together. I spent most of my time in the Army in the transportation division, and I drove trucks and transported people and equipment. I got out of the Army at the age of twenty-two, and immediately went to truck driving school and got my CDL license.

After I went to truck driving school, and got my CDL license, it was easy for me to get a job. I had many Job offers. I picked the best offer I thought I had offered to me. This job involved making a run from Houston to Chicago twice a week. I delivered car and truck parts for General Motors.

I never found time for a family. I figured I would have to spend too much time away from home to keep a wife happy and satisfied. I did meet many lonely women along the way, especially lonely waitresses at truck stops, who just wanted someone to show them a good time. I was enjoying the companionship and camaraderie up and down the highway from Houston to Chicago. I was devoted to my career as a truck driver as much as most professionals are devoted to their career.

I never will forget this one young lady. I was parked at a truck stop trying to catch a few winks. It was about 10 o'clock on a Tuesday night. I caught a little sleep wherever and whenever I could. As a truck driver you get use to such things. I heard a knock on my cab door. This young lady was standing there knocking on my door. I opened it.

"How're you doing?" she asked.

"I'm just trying to get a little rest. I have a long drive to Chicago. What about you?"

"I'm fine. May I join you?"

"Sure, you can."

Having a suspicious nature, I thought it was some kind of set up. The police often ran such sting operations from time to time. I was stopped at a truck stop in Memphis, Tennessee.

"I'm just looking for a little company."

At the time I didn't know if she was a prostitute or just someone who was very lonely, I could take the situation either way. I had picked up more than one prostitute in my day. She didn't seem too particular about her company, but only wanted a man.

"Get in," I said.

She was too elegant and classy to be a prostitute. She had on a nice gold watch; expensive gold earrings, a gold necklace and bracelet; a nice blue dress and beige shoes; and every strand of her hair was in place. She also had a beautiful face. She carried herself like Miss. Universe. I could tell she was only looking for someone to drive away the lonesome blues and wasn't a prostitute or a policeman. We sat and talked for at least an hour.

"Where're you from?" she asked.

"East Texas," I said. "That's over close to the Arkansas, Louisiana, and Texas border; a small town called Hallsville."

"How long have you been driving?"

"I've been driving for five years, this same run to Chicago."

"What kind of work do you do?"

"I'm a salesgirl at a department store."

"What brought you to the truck stop?"

"I hadn't had any luck with men in the past few years. Thought I'd find an interesting one at the truck stop."

"Well! did you?"

"I think so. I'm not sure yet."

"What're you exactly looking for?"

"Just someone I can talk to. The last man I had would have sex and leave. He never wanted to talk. He would only show up again the next time he wanted to have sex. And we couldn't have sex until he was inebriated. He reminded me much of my alcoholic father."

"Oh! that kind."

"How often do you make this run to Chicago?"

"Twice a week."

"I'd like to go to Chicago with you sometimes. I've never been out of Memphis."

"I suppose that could be arranged. Call me on my truck phone when you are ready to make the trip. I will stop here at the truck stop and pick you up." I gave her the number.

We had sex, and I gave her all the conversation she could stand for one night. The cab had plenty room to accommodate the sex act. I then told her I had to get on the road; I had parts to deliver. She acted sorry to see me go. She was the hungriest girl I had met in a long time. She was literally starved for affection and attention. I told her again to call me when she was ready to make the trip. She said she was off every Wednesday and Thursday.

She called me two weeks later and said she was ready to make the trip. I was making a trip to Chicago on the following Tuesday night, and set to return on Thursday night.

When I pulled up to the truck stop, she ran out with her bag and hugged me, as if she had missed me. It was my only stop on the way to Chicago. So, I went in and had a cheeseburger, fries, and Seven-Up, before getting on the way.

As we sat down at the booth, I noticed her perfectly

formed legs, her beautiful body, and her nice hair—as well as her overall immaculate appearance. I had my food, and we got on the road. She said she had already eaten. We got in the truck and got on the way. On the way there I tried to give her what she said she had been missing: plenty of conversation.

"Have you ever been married or engaged?" I asked.

"No, I haven't, have you?"

"No, I haven't either."

"What do you expect to see in Chicago?"

"I just want to see something different. Again, I get tired of seeing the same old things."

It took us eight hours to get to Chicago. We got a hotel room for the night, and we took in some of the sights.

I showed her Cubs and White Sox Park, Solider Field, Navy Pier, Buckingham Fountain, Sears Tower, Water Tower Place, the Museum of Science and Industry, the Shedd Aquarium, we explored the Loop area, and went to several nightclubs, including the Cotton Club. When we left, she said she was perfectly satisfied with her trip. She said it had been a long time since she had seen so much and had so much fun.

We kept our relationship up for the next ten years. We made an annual pilgrimage to Chicago once a year for the next ten years, and each time we tried to do and see something different. On the way back from what would be our last trip to Chicago, she said, "We've been seeing each other for a long time. Have you ever considered getting married, settling down, and raising a family?"

"I don't think that would be a good idea, since I'm on the road all the time. I wouldn't feel right leaving my wife at home while I'm driving up and down the road. Otherwise, I'd get married. I'd even marry you if you'd say yes."

"That flattering to know."

"Thanks."

Again, I was sacrificing my life as a family man for a career as a truck driver. My brother once told me that you should try to keep your life balanced. Don't get too heavily into one extreme or the other. I felt I was straying from his advice by focusing too much on my career and not enough on family. I finally figured out what he meant by trying to keep this balance and how important it was. A career man with no family can be very sad, and needless to say, a family man with no career is in trouble.

"Some men drive and manage a wife and family."

"Some do, but I don't believe I could."

"You should try it; you might like it. I would be the best wife there has ever been."

"Knowing you, I believe you. But I'm too old and set in my ways at this point."

She acted as if she was extremely disappointed in me.

"I've met someone, and we might get married. I wanted to give you the first offer."

During our trips to Chicago, she seemed to have been completely happy with me. I should have known she would eventually give up on me. They say you never miss your good thing 'till it's gone, and you never know what a good thing was until it walks away from you.

"I'm sorry, but I don't think I'm ready."

"If you ever feel ready, give me a call at this number."

I was sorry to disappoint her. But I had no intentions of changing my lifestyle. She gave me a business card and wrote her home number on it. We kissed for the last time and said our good-byes.

She called me several months later and told me she was getting married next month. She said we had some good times together, and she would cherish those times forever. She said she had never met anyone quite like me—that I was so real. I felt the same about her.

I asked her, "Would you consider moving to Texas and building a little house on a farm?"

"Sorry, too little too late. I've already made plans to get married. You should've said something several months ago, and I'd have gladly taken you up on your offer."

"Do you love him?" I asked.

"As much as any woman could love a man."

"You have my best regards."

"Thank you."

"Give me your address. I want to send you a gift."

"You don't have to do that."

"I love you also, and I want to do it. It'll be something for you to remember me by."

"I have enough of you to do that."

She gave me the address where I could send the wedding present. I didn't try to further talk her out of it. I knew any plans I could make would be tentative. It was the last I heard from her.

I kept making the trip to Chicago, but I never found anyone quite like her, even though I picked up a lovely waitress here and there. She left a tremendous cavity in my heart that I tried to fill with other lonely women. After five more years, I had a severe accident in my truck, on one cold and icy winter day in February, partially because of failing eyesight and hearing. My perception and reaction time weren't what they used to be. In addition, there was black ice covering the road for miles. The accident was unavoidable. I completely totaled the truck. The ice was the only thing I disliked about the run to Chicago. The company recommended that I retire.

I retired and built a nice little house on my family's homestead in East Texas. I hunted, fished, and went gambling in Shreveport when I had the cash. My grandniece passed away from cancer, and I took in one of her grandsons. I tried to raise him as best as I could. It was my contribution to family life. But nothing could fill the hole left in me by this sweet young thing. Although, she gave me every opportunity any man could ever have.

> *"Today, we must accept nothing but the best, and always be prepared for the worst."*
>
> *"It's in our nature to see what belongs to someone else in a better light than what belongs to us."*

═══ FOURTEEN ═══

Dream Collage

I frequently dream in collages of dreams: sometimes all in one night, and sometimes over a period of many nights. The dreams below were had by me over a long period of time, all of them with a consistent theme: the longing for being back home in East Texas. They seem rather unusual, since I have no burning desire to return to East Texas. I've had these dreams since living in the South Suburbs of Chicago over the past forty-six years. I frequently drift off to sleep and dream. Sometimes, I go from one dream directly into the other. On other occasions, I have a dream with a similar theme over time.

Vacation Home. We lived in a rusty-tin-roof shack in East Texas all during my youth. My nephew retired, hired a contractor to renovate and refurbish the shack, and moved back to East Texas to live. My nephew followed the current trend of some others, taking an old barn or building, renovating it, and making it into a superb living situation. That's exactly what he had done. He made it into a vacation home for the family. It was a beautiful place. It had all the modern conveniences: it had city water, natural gas, electricity, telephone services, and Internet connection. There was good fishing, hunting, and horseback riding. My nephew liked horses and like to ride them. He owned a stable full of horses. Family members would come, stay a few days, and hunt wild boar. The boar was numerous in the dense forest. We enjoyed hunting them with a bow and arrow. We made a fun sport of it. In my youth, to my knowledge, there were no wild boar running lose in the forest, but things had changed in many respects.

I dreamed once that I flew into Dallas/Ft. Worth, rented a car, and drove to East Texas. It was an easy drive: I took Interstate 20 out of Dallas to Hallsville, made a left on Farm Road 165 and went east. It took me about three hours to get there. My nephew gave me a party that Wednesday night before Thanksgiving in 1976. It was a cool and windy night, about 33 degrees.

He invited some of the neighborhood people. Some of them I had gone to school with. I got carried away with how well everyone was doing, got drunk on some good rye whiskey, and got into an argument with a neighbor I had gone to school with. I was a little jealous of how well everyone was doing. When I left in 1966, all the neighbors lived in shacks. Now those shacks had been replaced with fine-brick homes. They had heard from my nephew that I was doing well in Chicago and were jealous of me.

One of the neighbors asked me, "Where do you live in Chicago?"

"I live in a South Suburb of Chicago," I said.

"Oh! you're bigtime, you live in a south suburb."

As if to be sarcastic in a country boy way. And I didn't see where he was headed with the conversation.

"That's right," not responding to his sarcasm, I have a nice five-bedroom house in one of the better areas of the south suburbs."

"You really doing it then?

"You might say that."

"Drink some more whiskey," David said.

Not thinking he had anything planned, I kept drinking until I had a high blood/alcohol level.

"I see you guys in the neighborhood are doing OK, where do you work?"

"Most of us work at the electric plant in Longview."

"What about you?"

"I'm a teacher and a writer."

"Do you think you're better than we are?"

"No way man, we're all homeboys."

They were trying to pick a fight, and my nephew

was in on it. I hadn't expected such behavior from my nephew.

"You always did think you were better than the rest of us. You never ran around or drank with us, wouldn't let us ride in your car, and didn't hang around any of the community girls," David said.

I kept drinking one glass of whiskey after the other until I was stumbling and about to fall. My reaction time had gotten slower. When he saw that I was defenseless, he hit me with a sudden left, and knocked me on the couch. It was a sucker punch, and it was totally unexpected. I could barely get up, but I got up only to be hit with a right cross to the chest, before I could regain my balance, and this time fell backwards.

I heard a faint voice from my nephew say, "What're you trying to do, David, kill him? He's had enough."

"Just wanted to teach a Chicago boy a lesson," David said.

My nephew helped me to one of the spare bedrooms, and I fell asleep until the next morning. I got up wondering what happened; I was still dizzy and didn't realize what had happened.

I woke up from my dream wondering why I hadn't defended myself better. But realizing it was only a dream.

Black Soldier's Story. In another dream I had come home on a cool October day in 1976. For some reason, I was taking a walk through the neighborhood. One of my old friends stepped out of his house on his way up the road. He was walking tall and proud. He had on some type of soldier's uniform, with two gold bars on the shoulder, on the collar, and double stripes near the end of his sleeve. His shoes were spit-shined, and he looked very impressive. I had never seen him look so dapper. I hadn't seen him since he graduated high school, and I hadn't heard from him.

"What's up, Bubba?" I asked.

"What's going on, Craig?" he replied.

"What kind of uniform is that?"

"It's a National Guard's uniform."

"Isn't that an officer's uniform? How did you manage?"

Of all the uniforms I have seen us in, I had never seen one of us in a National Guard Officer's uniform.

"After bootcamp, I took the officer's test, and passed it with a high score. They sent me to Officer's Training School and made me an officer. I didn't join until three years after high school, but I'm glad I signed up."

"That's great man. I never could ace the test for an officer in the Navy."

Needless to say, I was jealous of him.

"I did all right, I was lucky, no big deal."

"What rank are you?"

"First Class Lieutenant."

I was jealous because it was my dream to wear a Lieutenant's uniform.

"I'm glad that one of us made it out of the ghetto."

"You did all right. My parents told me you were living in a bid house in Chicago."

"But I don't consider myself to have done as well as you, my brother."

Someone in the next house called him, and he said, "I have to go, see you later. Take care of yourself."

I woke up from my dream wondering why more Black soldiers couldn't become officers, and especially why I couldn't have been like Bubba.

Dream Come True. I had a dream that I was back in high school. It was a warm early April day in 1966. We were expecting the results of our ACT Test Scores. The principal came in our math class about ten o'clock and said the ACT Test Scores were back. The principal passed them out. I had made the highest score on the test of the students who took the test in our senior class.

I had had my scores sent to Howard University. The principal handed me a letter, along with my test scores. I had made 33 on the test. I think the highest possible score was 35. The letter said that I had been offered a full-ride to Howard. Several other students were planning on attending college, but none of them got scholarships. The next score to mine was 21, and then 16.

It was surprising because I wasn't the valedictorian or the salutatorian. I was only ranked number three in the class. We had a party that night to celebrate the college-bound seniors. There were four of us. We rented a room at the Holiday Inn in Longview, catered in some food, and bought some of the best whiskey we knew about. Anyone at the school could attend the party. We rented a double suite. We wanted to motivate others to follow in our footsteps.

We had a cross section of freshman, juniors, sophomores, and seniors. No one expected me to score that high on the ACT Test. I had a stutter in my speech, and never did talk much. Didn't participate in any student activities. One reason why I didn't participate in activities was because I lived at least twenty miles from the school. The only thing that personally saved me was that my brother-in-law would send me a new book every month starting in my freshman year. Sometimes I would go to Houston to visit my brother, stop in at one of the local bookstores, and pick up several books. I consistently had my head in a book.

I had dated this girl for two years; she was a sophomore. I started dating her when she was in the eighth grade. I was curious if she was going to wait for me until I graduated Howard University.

I got her in one of the corners of the suite, "Will you wait for me, Isabella?" I asked.

"You know I will, Larry," Isabella said.

"Washington, DC is a long ways away, and I might not get home too often."

"That's OK; I'll wait."

"If I can have you in my corner, I can make it."

"When will you be leaving?"

"I thought I would get an early start, go up for the summer, and get set up: I will use the summer to find a job, a decent apartment, and get to know the city."

I knew no one in Washington, DC or close to The District of Columbia. I would be strictly trying to make it on my own. I did have one advantage: my father had retired in 1962, and I was entitled to draw a small check every month until I turned twenty-three years of age— while in college. I couldn't let such an opportunity get away from me.

"You're leaving so soon?"

"I figure that's the best way to handle it."

"You must come home for Christmas. I hope to at least see you once or twice a year."

"Wild horses couldn't keep me away."

We all got drunk and had some good-old-clean country-boy fun.

I left that summer and went to Howard, found a decent apartment near campus, and got a job at a local Walmart. I came home only at Christmas. Isabella graduated in two years and followed me to Howard to matriculate. We kept my one-bedroom apartment, and she got a job waitressing in a local-posh restaurant. I graduated Howard and studied toward a Ph.D. in sociology at Howard. Isabella graduated Howard and became a math teacher. We bought a small house in Wilmington, Delaware, and both taught school: Isabella taught high school, and I taught sociology at a community college.

Again, I woke up to find it was only a dream. I slowly drifted back off to sleep.

State Championship. I never played much sports, either in the community, or on the playground at school. When the other boys were playing sports on the playground, I usually roamed around the campus. I never had toys to play with as a child, and my dexterity was underdeveloped. I also had poor hand-eye coordination. I was in the band through eighth grade, and the coach saw me as a "band-boy." As a freshman I asked the coach several times to let me play football. When I asked the coach to let me play as a freshman, he brushed me off. I didn't know anything about when and how tryouts for the various teams were held. My hand-eye coordination and my eyesight wouldn't allow me to play baseball. I did try basketball but ended up playing the last two minutes of every game. Part of the problem was that the coach simply didn't think favorably toward me. I never picked up a basketball before ninth grade. I had nowhere to practice and didn't have any equipment at home. Because of my late start and nowhere to practice, I got too late a start in basketball to be any good at it.

I could have participated in track and field, because I was quick as a rattlesnake. Again, when I approached the coach about track and field, I got the same brush-off. For some reason, he didn't want me playing on any of his sports teams. He was the only coach for four different sports: track and field, basketball, baseball, and football. These were the only sport the school competed in. If he didn't want you to play one sport, chances are you weren't going to play any sport. If he didn't like you, he just didn't like you. If each sport had had a different coach, I might have had a better earlier opportunity.

I dreamed the situation differently while lying in my bed in Chicago. As a junior, I had gained some weight and height. My friend was a star running back. He intervened for me and asked the coach to let me tryout. I tried out and became the second-string quarterback.

In the middle of the season the number one quarterback got hurt, and he didn't have any other choice but to put me in the game. I ran for two touchdowns during the second half of the game and threw for two touchdowns. From then on, I was the number one quarterback.

I got better and better in a short period of time. The position fit me like a customized glove. The coach did a 360 degree turn around with respect to me. I led the team to a State Championship in my junior and senior year. For the State Championship, I ran for two touchdowns and threw for three. We won the game 35 to 12, for the State Championship.

As a consequence of playing quarterback, the coach

let me participate in track and field. I recorded a 9.5 in the hundred-yard dash.

I was beginning to feel good about myself in that dream, but I woke up to the fact that I had only been dreaming.

Changes in the Old Homestead. I had another short dream about going back to my old homestead. I went back to East Texas on a cold and windy day in February 2000. My sister had told me that they had gotten city water, natural gas, telephone services, and Internet services. But I couldn't believe what I saw.

They had built a series of paved roads throughout the area, several different housing developments had gone up, with tree-lined parkways and curbs, storm drains, and sewers. They even had built a Walmart, McDonalds, and Home Depot in the local community. All these stores had a policy of not hiring from outside the community. There were plenty of jobs for people in the community. Streets were labeled, and there were road signs showing the way.

I decided it was time for me to make that move back to East Texas. But then I woke up and realized there had been some progress, but not that much. I turned over and went back to sleep.

> *"Having no options is a peculiar and desperate position."*
>
> *"The effects of your early programming will last a long time; even though you have moved beyond your early situation."*

FIFTEEN

Staying Out of Jail

My mother lacked many forms and kinds of information. She was born and lived most of her life at the end of one muddy trail or another; born before the automobile was invented. She only finished the eighth grade, and spent years on the family farm, until she was married at twenty-one-years old. Her mother died when she was eight. But one thing she told her sons: stay out of jail. Somehow, she knew how they treat you in jail, and how they label you once you have been in jail. This coming from a woman who had never been more than three-hundred miles from home. She was born in 1901, and most modern inventions came about during her lifetime: including the automobile, the airplane, and heating and air conditioning. Somehow, she never changed with the times, and kept doing things much as she had learned them in her childhood.

My mother wouldn't switch to an electric iron because she said it would get too hot. She used a mechanical lawn mower for years because she said a gas-powered mower would malfunction too readily. She said butane would blow up in your face: she resisted getting away from a wood stove and fireplace in favor of using butane. We tried to get my mother to invest in a tractor, rather than keep utilizing a mule to plow the fields, but she wanted nothing to do with such a mechanical plow. For my mother, inventions were slow to diffuse her existence.

Yet, she admonished her sons to stay out of jail. I took her advice, and I think most of my brothers and sisters did the best they could to follow her advice.

My mother even went further than just giving advice: her objective was to keep her sons occupied on the farm, in part to keep them busy and out of the devil's hands. In that way they wouldn't end up in mischief or jail. In that way she kept them plowing a mule from sunup to sunset, and doing other chores, for the balance of every day. Indeed, she kept them down on the farm. She felt that *an idle mind was the devil's workshop.* My father spent most of his time on the Gulf Coast. I never heard him discuss the issue of jail. He was brought up much as my mother, but was more up-to-date than my mother, yet he never challenged my mother's old-fashion ways. He tried to indulge her in every way he could. She also allowed him to indulge himself. They were complicit in each other's behavior.

One thing that helped me stay out of jail was some experiences I had as a youth. I saw my younger brother shoot my oldest brother with a handgun. I was seven years old at the time. I swore to never be violent to anyone. On another occasion, I saw my older friend hit a guy in the head with a chair, causing him to have a concussion. It also cracked his skull. This further insulated me against violence. Once I saw a classmate stab a guy in the heart with a six-inch-blade jackknife, this pushed me even further away from violence. I once witnessed a man shoot down a friend of mine like a rabid dog in the streets. Once I was sitting next to a friend in a restaurant when the friend got shot in the shoulder. During this time, I was assaulted by a much older classmate. This put the finishing touches on my nonviolent tendencies. Prior to seeing my younger brother shoot my oldest brother, I would fight at the drop of a hat, but since that time, I have always been slow to anger.

My oldest and my younger brother came home for Thanksgiving; this was soon after they constructed the graded-dirt road to our house. They got in an argument because my younger brother had loaned my oldest brother $500.00. They were both living on the Gulf Coast. My oldest brother was married and had three children. It seems that they started arguing over the money on the Gulf Coast several days before arriving in East Texas. They both were drinking heavily from a quart of Jack Daniels. They both got inebriated, and the argument started again.

"I need my money, man," Brent told Craig.

"Are you going to try and get blood from a turnip?" Craig replied.

Craig knew he had Brent over a barrel.

"Why did you borrow it if you knew you would have a hard time paying it back?"

"I thought I'd have it, and at the time was in a lot of trouble."

"Can't you give me something. I'm not asking for the entire amount?"

"You're a chicken shit Negro. You can't loan your own brother a few dollars without wanting it back the next day."

"What did you say?" Brent asked.

"I said you're a chicken-shit Negro," said Craig.

When Craig finished the statement; Brent reached in his pocket, pulled out a .38 Special, and shot Craig in the lower part of his abdomen. He was aiming for his heart. My mother used bandages to stop the bleeding, and my other brother immediately took Craig to the Negro hospital in Marshall. The hospital kept him for several day and then released him.

I went to visit my father on the Gulf Coast. He enlisted the services of a friend's son to watch me while he was at work. We went to play Ping-Pong at the community center. We both signed up to play. From the looks of things, we were both up next. My friend, Joseph, was smaller than the other guy who was about to challenge him.

The guy said, "I'm up next."

This guy must have been feeling his oats that day and thought he could intimidate Joseph because he was much bigger.

"We're up next," Joseph said.

"Says who?" the other guy said and picked up the ball and paddle.

Joseph simply picked up a chair and hit him in the head before he realized what was happening. They had to rush him to the hospital; his head was bleeding profusely. My friend, after hitting the guy, ran home, and left me there to deal with the aftermath.

Joseph's mother came over to my father's place that evening, and said the police were looking for him. Joseph had taken refuge in his girlfriend's house. It was summer and Joseph had to do a month in juvenile detention. When Joseph got out of detention, my vacation was over. I had gone back to East Texas. That scene of Joseph hitting that guy with the chair, and the blood oozing from his head, stayed with me for a long time. Sometimes I still have nightmares about it.

There was a dance at our school. These two boys, Jeff and Robert, had been arguing for days over Cecilia. I'm not sure why she didn't bring some closure to one of the relationships, and let them both know where they stood, but she was for some reason trying to keep them both hanging on. Cecilia was a beautiful and popular girl who was known for her flippant ways. These boys weren't the first to be led on by her. About halfway through the dance the disagreements came to a boil.

"Didn't I tell you to stay away from my girl?" Jeff said.

"What do you mean, your girl?" replied Robert.

"She told me she was my girl."

"You better stay away from her or something bad is going to happen to you."

"Are you threatening me?" Asked Jeff.

Jeff a was much bigger guy than Robert. Jeff stood six two and was muscular; he weighed about 180 lbs. Robert was five-ten, slender, and weighed only 150 lbs.

"I'm making you a promise."

"You keep dreaming. You better sit your little light behind down somewhere before you get hurt."

"You're the one that's dreaming."

"OK, let's take it outside."

Before Jeff could finish, Robert had punctured his Left vena cava with a six-inch-blade jackknife.

Jeff was taken to the Negro hospital in Marshall, Texas, but did not survive the night. Some of the blood from the stabbing jumped on my white shirt; I was standing just that close. As his heart was pumping the blood to the rest of his body, it had a powerful thrust. Robert did time as a juvenile for murder.

Freddie, a friend of mine in high school, wanted to visit a girl friend of his. He asked me to take him. I didn't know that her father had told Freddie, if he comes to his house again, he was going to kill him. I guess Freddie didn't believe him. We pulled up in front of the house, and Freddie got out and went to the door. The man must have looked out the window and saw it was Freddie. The man got a "12-gauge" shotgun, and shot Freddie in the chest and face, instantly killing him. The ambulance was called for Freddie by the girl's mother, but it was too late, he was dead on arrival. They had to have a closed casket, because the buck shots disfigured his face so badly. I was lucky the man didn't go berserk and shoot me as well, since I transported him.

I went to Tyler, Texas with some of my homeboys. They all had girlfriends in Tyler. We stopped at a local eating establishment. I was sixteen. It was the first and only time I ran with these homeboys. The owner of the restaurant had apparently told my homeboys not to come back in his place again. Of course, I didn't know about these admonitions. The owner wouldn't serve us. My homeys got angry began to throw things. The owners came out, and one of them came toward our table.

"We want something to eat," Tommy said.

"I told you guys that you were too rowdy, and never to come in my place again," the owner said.

"But we didn't do anything," Tommy Said.

Tommy was the oldest and was speaking for the group. The café had the best food in Tyler; it was especially known for its sandwiches.

"You had better get out of here or there's going to be trouble," the owner answered.

The owner came to our table. Tommy swung at him, and the owner pulled out a .32 caliber pistol and shot him in the shoulder. Tommy was in the hospital for several days but came out of it OK. I never will forget the look on Tommy's face when the bullet hit him. It was like everything stood still. It was the last time I traveled with my homeys. I knew my homeboys had a tendency to engage in violence on occasions, and this was not something I wanted to be a part of, so I moved on.

Because of these and other violent situations, I decided to stay away from violence, and thus out of jail. Engaging in violence is the easiest way I know to end up in jail.

In high school I drank at social events, mainly because of problems I had at home. But it never got bad enough for me to end up in jail. People knew I drank to deal with my problems. No one ever said anything to me about my drinking. I was once stopped by the highway patrol, but I was fortunate he let me off with a warning. I'm sure the people at school felt I was on the way toward becoming a drunk.

Only once in college did I get close to being placed

in jail. I was frustrated. The social scene was not what I desired it to be. I was so frustrated as a junior in college, that we were all sitting around the student center one day, and there was a paint can filled with black spray paint lying on the ground. I picked it up and painted the first letter of my name on the building. I guess I was trying to say I had been through the campus. I was a young ambitious lad, and felt I wasn't making the kind of name I should have been making for myself. When I put my initial on the building, in my mind at the time, it was in place of a more desirable impact.

The next day the police came to my dorm and knocked on the door. I opened the door.

"Are you Sean Crosby," the policeman asked.

"Yes, I am," I said.

"Come with me to the police station. You have to answer a few questions."

He escorted me across the campus and through the Student Center. I was overwhelmed with embarrassment. I rode to the station without saying a word.

"What's this all about, sir?"

I still wasn't sure what he wanted with me. After we got to the station, he posed some more questions. I also had a question.

"We got a report that you sprayed some graffiti on the Student Center."

"Yes, I sprayed the first letter of my name on the building."

He had me dead-to-right. I couldn't deny it. One of the college employees had seen me do it.

"That falls under the heading of destruction of property."

He told me I had to pay a fifty-dollar fine or spend a night in jail. I was lucky enough to get one of my professors to pay the fine. It's the only thing that kept me from spending a night in jail.

Since that time, I have been careful about my behavior, and always try to do like my mother advised: stay out of jail. Throughout my life, I have figured that I should cling to every bit of wisdom my mother gave me. My mother didn't hand out words of wisdom too often, and when she did, I felt I had better heed it.

I avoided violence, and that one thing I believe has so far kept me out of jail. With that and the help of the Good Lord! I have never spent a single night in jail. I didn't think I could take much of visiting hours, institution food, close quarters, and being blocked from the sun. For these reasons and more, I decided I didn't like jail.

Of course, there are many other activities that can land you in jail. But in avoiding violence, I managed to stay away from the most accessible avenue to a jail cell.

SIXTEEN

Narrow Escape

I was born Carlos Lewis Crosby on November 16, 1947, on a cold fall night. I had four brothers and five sisters. My nephew was born Craig Grant Hightower on October 25, 1949. He only had a much older brother. I was sixteen and Craig was fourteen. We lived in a rural area of Hallsville, Texas. Craig was my oldest sister's son.

I was five-six, about one-hundred-twenty-five pounds, with caramel skin. Craig was five-four, one-hundred-twenty pounds, with a shade darker skin than mine. He had lived in Houston all his life, and I had lived in the country for all mine. I had attended inferior schools all of my life, and Craig had mostly attended excellent schools. I had received little or no encouragement from parents, siblings, relatives, significant others, teachers, preachers, or the community; Craig had received every possible support from these sources. His education and background were far superior to mine, yet he was virtually afraid of his shadow.

Once in first grade Craig was visiting us and said, "I'm 'king-on-the-throne.'"

I said, "You made that up, there's no such thing as a 'king-on-the-throne.'"

I knew how creative Craig's mind could get. I knew making up things wasn't unusual for him. He once told me that a certain candy made you strong like superman.

"Yes, it is," he said.

"Why hadn't I heard about it then?"

"Don't you look at TV?"

That's how bad my education was. I was in third grade and had never heard of a "king-on-the-throne." My mother watched only what she wanted to watch, and the TV was her constant source of entertainment. The only time I watched TV was when I watched what my mother wanted to watch. This left me unexposed in many ways. A second TV was unheard of for a family in my area of the country in those days.

Again, Craig once asked me when he was in first grade, and I was a third grader, "What is the capital of Texas?"

"What do you mean by capital?"

"Every state in the United States has a capital."

"I never heard of that."

"Austin is the capital of Texas."

"I guess I do need to attend a better school."

"There are a lot of good schools in Houston. You could live with us if you wanted."

"My mother and father need me, I have to stay with them, and get whatever education I can."

The only reason I didn't ask my mother and father if I could make the change was because I knew they needed me. I was the only male in the household besides my father, and my father spent most of his time on the Gulf Coast. He only came home twice a month. My mother and I had to run the farm.

Once more, Craig asked me when I was in third grade, and he was in first grade, "Did you know a caterpillar turns into a butterfly?"

I had heard of a butterfly, but didn't know what a caterpillar was. As a country boy, I should have been familiar with that process.

"What's a caterpillar?" I asked.

"You don't know anything. What do they teach you in school?"

"They teach me what I need to know."

At that time, I felt the need to get defensive.

Craig told his mother, "Carlos doesn't know that a caterpillar turns into a butterfly."

"That's all right, Craig, when I was his age, I probably didn't know it either."

I appreciated my sister standing up for me. But still

felt Craig was right: my education was lacking to a great degree.

"Maybe you're right," Craig said to his mother, "I guess there're lot of things I don't know as well, compared to some other people."

From that point on, I kept my nose to the grindstone, trying to learn everything I could. My brother-in-law was a teacher, and I borrowed books from him. I asked people to buy me books for my birthday and Christmas rather than other types of gifts. When I visited any large city, the first place I went was the book store or library. I bought a TV so I could watch educational programs. By my sixteenth birthday, my knowledge of most things was superior to Craig's.

We lived twenty miles from Marshall (25,000); Hallsville was twenty miles away (1,300); we were thirty miles from Longview (42,000); one-hundred-forty-five miles from Dallas (700,000); Shreveport, Louisiana was fifty miles to the south (165,373); Tyler was 60 miles to the north (52,000); Kilgore was 40 miles north (12,000); Harleton was seven miles east (1,000); and Jefferson was 20 miles further east (3,200).

Until the dirt road was constructed in 1954, we didn't have electricity. We got butane when I was a freshman in high school; a telephone when I was a junior in college; and a pump put in our well after I had left home for a number of years. The dirt road was hot and dusty in summer and muddy in winter. Once while transporting my mother to church, after a drenching rain, the car became immobilized in a foot of red clay. This dirt road led to a winding, curvaceous, and hill-ridden highway. This highway in one direction led to Marshall, and in the other direction led to Hallsville and Longview. They did pave the road before I graduated high school, but the pavement soon wore off due to a lack of maintenance.

My parents had to walk for miles in order to get to school. When they got to school, they found it heated by a potbellied stove, the building about to fall down, wind coming in through the cracks in winter, and inadequate books and supplies, as well as curriculum. My parents didn't encourage my education; nor did my sisters, brothers, relatives, teachers, significant others, or community people. There were no books in our home except the Bible. Someone once brought a copy of *Paradise Lost* and left it at our house: I must have read it a million times. Not only did my parents not encourage my getting an education, in fact, in numerous ways, my parents tried to discourage me from pursuing an education.

My mother caught me reading early one morning before school, on a bright sunny April day, and made me get up and plow for a few days before boarding the bus to school. She said that if I had time to read, I had time to plow. She insisted that time at home was for doing chores, and that I should do my schoolwork at school. I felt she was trying to get me to drop out without actually verbalizing it. When I learned to drive, on any number of occasions, she had me miss school to transport her for personal business. She had no other way of getting where she wanted to go. Neither my mother or father ever learned to drive.

It was now August of 1963. Craig had come from Houston to spend his usual summer vacation with us. We lived on a farm, and Craig enjoyed getting out of the city and getting some of that clean-fresh air that is so common in the country. His mother and father also wanted to get him from under the influence of gangs and other incorrigibles. His allergy attacks also seemed to come less frequently. All the work was done on the farm for the summer, and nothing was left but the harvest. We never asked Craig to lift a finger around the farm.

Craig specifically liked Alberta peaches. I favored them myself. I told him that I knew exactly where there were some growing. There was an old homestead nearby where a cousin used to live, but had moved to California. Most of the old-timers were moving out and others were moving in: they headed for larger cities. There were still some Alberta peach trees on the property where the house once stood. Craig liked them because they were usually big, sweet, ripe, and juicy during this time of the year. So, we decided to venture by the old homestead to see if we could find some.

We had peaches of one kind or another but none

compared to Alberta peaches. He specifically wanted Alberta peaches, and Craig was spoiled and use to getting what he wanted. I had no choice but to try and appease his appetite.

We got up that morning and had some fresh milk (the milk came from a cow in the pasture), sausage (the sausage came from a hog we raised and slaughtered), pancakes, and grits; we then got on our way. It was only a trail leading through the woods to the old homestead where we wanted to go. At one time there were no roads at all; only a series of muddy trails connecting the residents of the community to one another. There was a new subdivision near this old homestead, but they didn't see fit to connect it to the road that led to our house. We got on the trail and was there in a matter of minutes.

Wandering through the trail we saw snakes, foxes, coyotes, squirrels, raccoon, possums, and other small animals crossing the trail. Craig was fearful of these animals, especially snakes. He had never seen such animals except in a zoo. A rattlesnake was lying near the trail, and Craig was afraid, but I convinced him to forget his fears and keep moving. The rattlesnake crawled away when we got close. He was even afraid of cows and horses. Horses and cows were grazing nearby the trail, and Craig became afraid they would run after him. I told him if he didn't bother them, they wouldn't bother him.

As we walked along the trail to the old homestead, Craig asked, "Don't you get tired of these woods?"

"It's home, and I'm used to it. You get used to it like anything else. If you live long enough under any given set of conditions you can get use to them."

"Again, he reminded me, I guess you're right. But you could come to live with us in Houston. I have a bunkbed in my room that you could use."

I reminded him, "My family needs me on the farm."

"You're right about that. I hadn't thought seriously about that, even though you mentioned it before."

"I'm sure if you ever changed your mind and decided to come, my parents would be agreeable and accommodating."

"Thanks a lot. It's a good thing to know that I always have an alternative."

"There are good schools, libraries, book-stores, and girls everywhere,"

"That sounds good."

"I know you'd like it."

"If it's so good, why do you spend you summer vacations with us?"

"Just good to get away for a while."

"You could spend it somewhere else other than the country, and probably find it much more enjoyable."

"But this place is different. No other place like it. In addition, I get to harass you."

"I believe you're right about that."

We came to a creek with a log thrown across it from one side to the other. Craig was afraid to walk across the log to get to the other side, afraid he might fall into the water (the water was deep enough to be over his head, there was reason to fear), but I convinced him to cross it. We came to a fence and Craig had difficulty getting over the fence, but with some coaching, he made it through OK without cutting himself on the barbed wire.

There were several trees of Alberta peaches and no one to tell us we couldn't have them. The old house that once sat on the property had been torn down. The only reminder that a house once stood there was an old chimney. We simply sat there on that chimney and ate until our hearts were content. The peaches were more delicious than they had ever been before. I believe that for once Craig was completely satisfied.

When we had had our fill, as boys will do, we decided to wander through the new subdivision that was about one-hundred feet up the trail. In the new subdivision there were many new brick, multi-level structures; with curbs, gutters, and tree-lined parkways. There were also modern paved streets and paved driveways. Prior to other groups moving in we only had dirt roads. Since they moved in the dirt roads were paved.

We wandered through the subdivision for a short while until a man in an F-100, red, 1962, Ford pickup spotted us, pulled up to us, rolled down his window, and asked, "Where are you boys headed?"

"Just walking."

We started running. He got out of his truck and ran after us, but he was no match for two desperate teenagers, who knew the landscape, and were full of energy.

"Come back here," he said.

We didn't have any better answer than that, and figured being young and full of energy, we could outrun him and get to the trail. We cut through someone's yard and headed for the trail with all the speed we could muster. We ran until we got to the trail and headed to our house. We knew we had to cross a creek and several fences, and that he couldn't possibly follow us in his truck. In addition, the woods were too thick. We kept going at top speed until we got near our house. We then slowed down and relaxed. I was worried about Craig because of his allergies, but he ran faster than I. Craig had frequent attacks of his allergies which wouldn't allow him to physically exhaust himself, but his allergies didn't seem to bother him during his escape.

My parents had warned us before to stay clear of the new subdivision, but as teenagers will do, we had to test our mettle. People in the new subdivision seem to feel we were the intruders, when if anyone was invading it was them.

We never came back for more Alberta peaches, and were thankful to have made that narrow escape. We knew it was dangerous to venture as far as the new subdivision, and from that point on stayed clear of it.

SEVENTEEN

Jealousy and Envy

My brother Henry had left a 1951 Fleetline Chevrolet
sitting in a run-down, deteriorated, and dilapidated-
old shed, about fifty feet from the house, when I was
thirteen. He had begun teaching me how to drive when
I was eleven, but decided he wanted to move back to
the Gulf Coast. No reasons were given as to why he
was abruptly leaving. Some say he was getting away
because he had gotten a young girl pregnant. Henry
was a little unstable and didn't stay anywhere very long.
He had only been in East Texas a few years. The car
had a lot of play in the steering wheel and needed some
struts. You had to make allowances for the play in the
steering column. The engine was also about shot. After
he left, I would get in that old 1951 Fleetline Chevrolet
and drive where I wanted to go, until Henry sold it to

my older brother, Sam. Sam wanted the car for his two children. Before Sam bought it, I had begun, even at thirteen, to roam all over the countryside. At thirteen I had started driving it to town and to school, with no fear of the police. Henry did warn me to watch out for the police, but at that age I had no fear of them. After Sam purchased the car from Henry, I then had nothing to drive for a while.

From the time Henry sold the 1951 Fleetline Chevrolet to Sam, when I was thirteen, I had to go where I wanted to go by hook or crook until I turned eighteen. At times I had to strike out on foot. That included going to town (usually you could catch a ride with a neighbor), getting to school activities (sometimes the school bus would take us to school activities), and going on dates (going on dates was the most difficult feat to accomplish, and usually I stayed at home). When my brother purchased the car for me a burden was seemingly lifted off my shoulders.

It was March 1966. I was a senior in high school. When I was eighteen, and had gotten my driver's license, Henry purchased me a 1964 Bell-Aire Chevrolet. It had a 327 engine, was maroon, with an automatic transmission, black interior with bubble-plastic covering the seats, chrome rims, and two pipes coming out the back. The engine was perfectly sound. It was something to behold, and was almost the perfect toy. Lots of people were extremely jealous and envious of my car. Some would tell you they were jealous while others were subtle about it. Most parents or relatives couldn't afford to purchase their son or daughter such a car. No one in my class, except me, was able to drive such a car of his own. When I got the car, I became virtually independent: I could come and go as I pleased. My father had retired when I was sixteen. That meant I received a Social Security check of my own. So, I had a car and cash to buy what I wanted. No one knew about the check I was getting, otherwise I guess they really would have been seriously jealous.

I didn't realize that jealousy and envy was so strong in young people. I always believed in *live and let live*. I never felt one way or the other about material things that belonged to another person. Even if I wished I owned such things, I never resented them for what they had. My philosophy was, "more power to an individual if they were fortunate enough to acquire some material things." Apparently, other people felt differently about the issue. I found out that when one person is seemingly doing well, it brings haters out of the woodwork.

There was a student in my class who resented me for the way I dressed and the car I drove. I mostly wore designer clothes from specialty shops. Jambone was also jealous because I made better grades than he did in math, on the ACT Test, and that I had voiced my ambition for going to college. He was an older student; and had been to prison, reform school, had even tried the army, and was returning to school trying to get a high school diploma. He attacked me one day in the fieldhouse. He put his hand in my collar. He was five-eight, 170 lbs., muscular, and athletic. I was five-five, 125 lbs., frail, and without much muscle mass. I found out later that he already had gotten a GED, but his dream was to play sports in high school. I once heard him say, he'd rather play sports than eat.

I had seen him earlier that day take a carton of Marlboro cigarettes from the vendor who was responsible for putting candy in the machine. I guess Jambone was feeling bold that day. He was usually not that obvious in his criminal behavior. He passed by the station wagon and saw the cigarettes lying on the back seat. He then, as quick as lightning, opened the door, grabbed the cigarettes, and ran for the fieldhouse up the hill. Jambone must have truly been having a nicotine fit. He was risking his good status as a student and athlete.

As he cuffed me, he said, "You better not tell on me."

"I don't care what you do," I said.

"If you do, I'll get you."

"Don't worry."

"You won't be safe anywhere you go."

He picked me off the floor again. Tears almost coming to my eyes. I was afraid of what this powerful street guy could do to me. Once Jambone got you down there was no getting up.

The next day we were standing around the front of the school before class. One guy, Antoine, who was big and strong, and had been retained in the twelfth grade several years, called me to the side like he wanted to tell me something. But before he could tell me, Jambone, who had grabbed me in the collar the previous day, all of a sudden hit him across the face, and they got into a scuffle. Jambone threatened him, saying he better not tell me about it. He pushed Antoine around like he was as light as a feather.

A friend of mine told me that Antoine had seen Jambone do something to my car, and was going to tell me about it, but Jambone picked a fight with him to divert his attention and prevent Antoine from telling me. The friend said Jambone had put a foreign substance in my gas tank. All the boys knew what Jambone had put in my gas tank. I kept driving the car and never said anything to him about it. You had to be careful in dealing with Jambone; he wasn't beyond murder. I heard he went to prison for attempting to murder his stepfather. He shot him with a .45 caliber pistol. This was the beginning of my car taking a turn for the worse; and I did notice the car never did run properly after that. I never did know for sure what he had put into my gas tank. I didn't know he was that jealous, but I knew he was somewhat jealous of my car and my academic standing. He put in his high school memory book that I was most likely to not succeed.

Jambone had a lot of people fooled. But I knew he was a thug, a thief, and criminal who would do anything to achieve his objectives. We both moved on to do what each of us had to do with our lives. After high school, I never heard from Jambone again. One friend did mention his name, but I didn't pay a lot of attention to what he was saying about him.

My house was the last house on the road where I lived. Other boys in the community were jealous of my car, that I was a serious student, and the fact that I didn't ride them around with me. I usually picked up my girlfriend and took her with me everywhere I went, and there was no space for onlookers or stragglers. My brother had made it a condition of giving me the car, that I not ride a bunch of guys, up to no good, up and down the highway. But they thought, because I didn't haul them up and down the highway, that I felt I was better than they were. They also thought I felt I was better than they were because I never gave one thought to dropping out of school. Most of them dropped out as a freshman or sophomore—sometimes even before that.

One day I tried to start up my car and it caught fire. Once I put out the fire, I noticed the gas filter was broken, as if it had been deliberately done. The material in the filter was too strong to break without some help.

Some of the neighborhood boys were pretty smart about cars. I believe someone busted the gas filter so the car would catch fire. Sand was the only thing I had available to put the fire out. My car never did run right after it caught fire. I have no idea how much damage the sand did.

About a week later, I put an old childhood friend out of my car. He refused to put any gas in my car. When I did ride someone in my car, I demanded that they put some gas in it. The gas was costing me, and I wasn't about to give out any freebies. We had been friends for a long time. We had both used my truck to haul hay for a nearby farmer. I had paid Bucko from the money I had gotten. But he said he didn't have any money. I put him out in Longview, about 20 miles from our homes in the country. I figured he was only trying to use me.

Another friend of mine told me that Bucko had come back in the middle of the night, several days later, and put something in my gas tank. The neighborhood boys had advised him what to put in it to disable the engine. Bucko wouldn't have known what to do on his own. He didn't know one end of a car from the other. The shed wasn't locked, and stood away from the house. Anyone could approach under cover of night and do whatever they wanted. We had a habit of not getting up once we had gone to bed. I never knew what Bucko did, but noticed my oil became blackened, and soon my rings began to leak oil on the spark plugs. This is where I completely lost friendship with Bucko.

My car was running poorly, but I was still trying to date this young lady. Her brother wasn't fond of me; nor were her mother, father, brother, sister, aunts or uncles. Someone told me that while I was inside seeing his sister, Jayson put sand and gravel in my gas tank. In addition, a friend of mine was home from college, and wanted to visit his girlfriend. I knew how he felt, but didn't want to leave my girlfriend's home, and told him he could drive my car to see his girlfriend. It was foolish of me; I didn't even know if he could drive it. Many of those who can drive an automatic can't drive a standard-shift. But I didn't even ask him if he could drive it, I simply gave him the key. I heard that his girlfriend's brother had a strong dislike for me, and put some sand into my gas tank. These were only rumors, and I never had any proof of any of it, but my car began to run worse and worse. After the friend brought it back it even sounded louder, as if something was badly wrong with it.

Another guy who wasn't even a student at the high school I attended was jealous of my car. Someone said they saw him fooling around with my car in the school's parking lot. I believe he did something, though I have no idea what it was. Some of the country boys knew exactly what to do to disabled a car. This individual had dropped out of high school, was working, and still couldn't afford to buy a car like mine. That's what he was jealous of. He was also jealous of the fact that I was still in school and he had dropped out.

I had gone to see my brother in Longview, Texas the previous summer, and met a young man who was mostly a thug, a thief, and a drug addict. I went back to visit my brother. This thug came over to see how I was doing. I acted like I didn't want to be bothered with him. That night a neighbor said he saw Clay fooling around with my car. I don't know what he did, if anything, but after that the car never ran decently. It was barely tinkering along, but after that it completely quit functioning properly.

I once visited a neighbor. My father wanted to visit. I walked into the house, but felt uneasy, and came back outside. One of the young boys was standing there by my tank with a handful of sand. I didn't know if he had an opportunity to put any in my tank, but believe that was his intentions. It's almost like being hunted without any real reason or rhyme.

It was time for me to go to college. I didn't figure the car would last much longer. I didn't want to be bothered with an old car in college. I didn't want anything to interfere with my studies. All I knew to do was to give it back to Henry. I should have tried to get Henry to trade it in on a newer model, but didn't. I was lucky the car made it to Houston. It stopped several times, but I was able to get it started again. While most of the boys in my community wanted to get a car, a job, an apartment, and a degree of independence from their families; I was interested in going to college and getting on with my life. I had already had all those things. I believe all these individuals collectively kept me from having a car of my own in college. If they hadn't damaged my car it would have lasted a long time.

After high school, I moved on. I haven't kept contact with many old friends or associates. I believe there is balance and justice in the universe, and everyone will have to eventually pay for their misdeeds, if the Almighty God sees that as being necessary.

> "School won't make you intelligent, but
> it can help to prepare you for life."
>
> "Some people will tell you what you can't
> do, but it's not important what you can't
> do, only important what you can do."

EIGHTEEN

Life on Our Farm

I resented many things about growing up on our small farm in East Texas, but I was kept busy, and always had plenty to eat. One thing I really disliked more than anything else was that for most of the time I was isolated without any means of transportation. I also didn't like plowing a mule from sunup to sundown in an age of jet propulsion. My mother had the right idea that keeping me busy would help to keep me out of trouble. It did keep me out of trouble, but it also limited me in many other respects. Since we grew our own food, we had ample food stuffs. Some people in our community were always scrounging for food. There were ten children in our family, and I was the youngest.

We lived in a rusty-tin-roof shack. When it rained water came through the roof. The wind could be felt coming through the cracks in winter time, and it was unbearably hot in summer. Winters seemed harsh only because we didn't have sufficient heat, and lived in such a drafty old house.

We were isolated for the most part, and limited in our interactions with others in the community. The only time we got a visit from a neighbor was when the neighbor needed a favor of some kind. There were no playing games or engaging in social activities with the neighbors. We lived at the end of a three-mile trail that led off a winding, curvaceous, and hill-ridden highway that meandered its way to small towns in either direction—north or south. Town in either direction was twenty miles away. Along this trail was a number of other families, though—again, we had little contact with them. I attribute part of my speech problem to being isolated along this trail as a youth, and my relatives not bothering with me because of my speech problem. We lived west of the main highway. Before the road was constructed, it was only a trail that led to our house. The trail had overhanging tree limbs and was narrow. Only someone in a wagon, on horseback, or on foot could navigate that grassy trail. In some places, ditches were as wide, and deep enough to hide a house. There were dew, mud, and wild animals along this trail: there was especially dew in the mornings, and mud after a rain.

After the road was constructed, it was muddy in winter, and dusty and sandy in summer. Sometimes the mud would get so deep after a rain that your car would get stuck. Once I was transporting my mother to church on a Sunday morning, in a 1951 Fleetline Chevrolet, at twelve years old, and my car became immobilized in a foot of red clay. Some boys who lived nearby helped to rescue and push us out of the mud. I got mud all over my shoes but continued on to church. In some places sand was deep, and in other places there were uneven places in the road.

I had to get up early and feed the chickens, ducks, guinea fowls, dogs, pigs, horses, and cows—every day. During growing season, I had to get up early before the sun would rise and plow until the sun would set. My parents were too out of date to buy a tractor, and preferred to keep using a plow and mule. Mostly every day during growing season I spent plowing that mule from sunup to sunset. It didn't get too hot for my mother, and you know how hot it gets in East Texas. Some days the temperature would reach 105 degrees, but I got no relief from plowing in the fields. My mother was seemingly convinced that the plow was the road to my salvation. Once I decided to discontinue working early, and my mother whipped me with a limb from a peach tree. Chickens, ducks, guinea fowls, and other animals ran freely and left their droppings in the yard. Rats ran freely throughout the house. Once my sister's boyfriend was visiting, and mice were playing on the family room floor, right in front of them, as if they owned the entire farm.

We had to work all the summer cultivating the soil. We began in March breaking up the ground and ended in fall with the harvest. In the fall we had to pick the dried peas, pull the corn, pull up the peanuts, dig up the sweet potatoes, and Irish potatoes, and pick the cotton. We didn't even have a wagon at this time like we once did, but had gotten a truck. We still had to somehow get our harvest to the barn.

My father worked on the Gulf Coast and only came home twice a month until he retired in 1962. My mother supervised the farm work. It was mostly on my shoulders. All my brothers had left for the Gulf Coast. It was a fifty-acre farm, and I had no one to help me. My sister and mother only did a little hoeing and cultivating. My father retired and came home when I was a sophomore in high school, and he then did some of the work. He bought a truck, and we would sell our produce by peddling them to people in nearby towns. I wanted to set up a roadside stand on one of the thoroughfares, to save wear and tear on the truck, but my father liked peddling from house to house. We had to get up early and get the produce ready for market. Again, we had to do it all, we had no one to help us. Some of it we did the evening before. I was able to earn enough money to buy school clothes and whatever else I needed from the money I earned selling vegetables from house to house.

My father would take one side of the street and I would take the other. The only problem I ever had was a man drew a knife on me and asked me to come to the back door. I went to the back door and he was satisfied. He even purchased some vegetables.

For most of my life on the farm we didn't have butane, natural gas, a telephone, or running water. We got electricity as soon as the road was constructed, butane when I was a freshman in high school, a telephone when I was a sophomore in college, and running water after I had graduated college and moved to Chicago. For my parents, invention and diffusion took place very slowly. Prior to getting electricity, the only energy we used was wood. We used wood in the fireplace and the stove. We used a coal oil lamp for lighting. We didn't know what a utility bill was at that time.

A big event of the year was hog-killing time, usually shortly before Christmas, and sometimes the Saturday before Christmas. We would fatten a hog all year long in preparation for the slaughter. We did it the old-fashioned way. We would gather up the wood required to provide enough hot water to remove the hair from the hog, cook off the cracklings, and make soap. We would eat these cracklings and use the soap for the rest of the year.

We would heat the water to its boiling point in large black pots to maximize the removal of the hair. The water would have to reach a scalding temperature. Someone would have to go down the hill to the pen and get the hog. Usually, the hog would physically resist, as if it knew what we had planned for it, and the end was near. We would tie a special knot in a rope and put the rope on its hind leg, so we could maintain control of the hog, and could then drive it up the hill. Usually, when we tried to hold one of its legs to slip on the rope, it would double-clutch kick, trying to prevent the rope from going on its leg. When we got the rope on, we would drive the hog up to where we could put it on a platform and get the hair off its body. We would get it close to where it would be slaughtered. When we drove the hog up the hill, usually it would try to get away, if possible. After getting the hog to where we wanted it, one of my brothers or my father would shoot it directly between the eyes, trying to hit it in the brain. Then my father or brother would stab it in the heart, right between the front legs. When the blood was drained from its body, we would lift it to a platform and begin the process of removing the hair.

Once the hair was removed, we would raise it on a scaffold and remove the entrails. We would then lower its body to a table and cut it into various sections of meat. My brother and father were both good at butchering. The women would then clean the chitterlings, make the hog-head cheese, and cut up the meat for cracklings and sausage. A small amount of the fat would be used to make soap. It takes a lot of water to clean chitterlings.

My job was to keep the fire burning so that all of

these activities could go off smoothly. Another job for me was to grind the sausage. Certain parts of the lean meat were used to make sausage. Most people only see bacon, sausage, neckbone, pig's feet, ham, and pork chops in the grocery store, and never give much thought to how it got to the store. Before we got electricity and got a freezer, we would pack our meat in a big box of salt. We would have plenty of meat to eat for a while. I can remember only once killing a calf. But we killed a hog at least once a year. After I moved to Chicago, I heard the state would not allow people to butcher their own cows and hogs anymore. I believe the state considered it to be too many health considerations to allow it to go on.

For a long time, we had to get our water from a spring up the hill. It was too much trouble to carry water for washing down the hill. We finally had a well dug. We didn't get a pump put in the well until I was out of college and working in Chicago. We didn't even get an outhouse until I was a freshman in high school. Before the outhouse, any grove of trees served as a bathroom and protection from onlookers. The outhouse was no good at night because it sat at least one-hundred feet from the house, right next to the forest.

I had to take out every morning, wash, and at night bring in my mother's chamber pot. I used to hate washing it out and bringing it in to her bedside. Sometimes when I took it out it would smell awful—naturally.

At the beginning of my education, I had to walk

that three-mile dirt road to the bus stop. It was rough sometimes after a rain and on cold-frosty mornings. When I got in about third grade, the bus started picking us up at our front door. Once I got to school, I was exposed to an inferior education. The school functioned from a shoestring budget and was limited in terms of curriculum. But we did manage to get in a little education, even though it was inadequate with respect to the mainstream culture. We rarely read an outside novel, wrote a paper, or even practiced writing. We all received limited academic preparation, though some of our educations were better than others. We weren't prepared for anything but sweeping floors in some factory, the job that was so common for many of us.

I was happy to get my high school diploma and move on to bigger and better things. My parents couldn't afford to send me to college, but after my father retired, I was able to draw a check from Social Security—if I continued in school. I could draw that check until I graduated college, or until my 23rd birthday, whichever came first. I took advantage of that fact, because I knew it was a chance of a lifetime, and a chance that many people could only hope for and dream about. I would have been a bumbling idiot, with no insight, not to take advantage of that opportunity. I was also able to get a student loan. I was so determined that I would have worked my way through college if there was no other way. I figured with my background I would need all the time I had for study purposes. I had seen the impact of total ignorance.

When I graduated high school, I was delighted to get away from that farm, and move on to college. I have often thought about returning to the old homestead, but have a lot of bad memories in regard to the farm.

My father and mother passed away in 1988 and 1989 respectively. All four of my brothers and two of my five sisters have passed away also. The family home has probably fallen down by this time. I hadn't been back to that part of the country since my mother died.

At this point, a lot of Blacks have moved out and other people are steadily moving in. I here they have pumped in city water, have good telephone service and Internet connection, and probably natural gas. They have also taken more interest in keeping the road paved.

As for me, I have learned to be thankful for the small things, and what I did have, rather than what I didn't have. My sister tells me that not many parents would have turned that entire Social Security check over to their child. And once my brother gave me the car in high school, I was able to go and come as I pleased. Most parents would have wanted more control. But at least I was able to get some degree of freedom and independence after getting in high school. I think my freedom and independence motivated me to attend college. Since I had already had a degree of freedom and independence, and a car, I wasn't dying to head to the big city and achieve those things. I was also lucky to have a brother who thought enough of me to encourage me early on when he thought I deserved it, to put money in my pocket, and to later give me a car.

It is now 2020. I live in a South Suburb of Chicago, had a decent career, have two sons who went to college, a good wife, a decent house, and two cars that provide good transportation. Overall, I consider myself fortunate. I could have been just another misfortunate brother.

ABOUT THE AUTHOR

JAY THOMAS WILLIS is a graduate of the University of Houston, Houston, Texas, where he earned a Masters' degree in social work; he is also a graduate of the Masters' degree counselling program at Texas Southern University, Houston, Texas. He attended undergraduate school at Stephen F. Austin State University, Nacogdoches, Texas, where he earned a B.S. degree in sociology and social and rehabilitative services.

He worked as a Clinical Social Worker for seventeen years, providing direct clinical services as well as supervision. He has been a consultant to a nursing home and a boys' group home; taught college courses in sociology, family, and social work in community college and university settings; and has worked as a family therapist for several agencies in the Chicago area. In addition, he was a consultant to a number of home-health care agencies in the south suburbs and Chicago.

Mr. Willis is a past CHAMPUS peer reviewer for the American Psychological Association and the American Psychiatric Association. He also spent a number of years in private practice as a Licensed Clinical Social Worker in the State of Illinois.

Mr. Willis has traveled and lectured extensively on the condition of the African American community. He has written twenty-eight books, and written many journal articles on the subject of the African American community. He has written several magazine articles. He has also written Op-Ed Commentaries for the *Chicago Defender*, *Final Call*, *East Side Daily News* of Cleveland, and *Dallas Examiner*. He currently lives in Richton Park, Illinois with his wife and son.

Printed in the United States
By Bookmasters